*COSTUMES
for
TIME
TRAVELERS*

COSTUMES
for

TIME TRAVELERS

A. R. CAPETTA

CANDLEWICK PRESS

This is a work of fiction. Names, characters, places, and incidents are either products of the author's imagination or, if real, are used fictitiously.

Copyright © 2025 by A. R. Capetta

All rights reserved. No part of this book may be reproduced, transmitted, or stored in an information retrieval system in any form or by any means, graphic, electronic, or mechanical, including photocopying, taping, and recording, without prior written permission from the publisher.

First edition 2025

Library of Congress Control Number: 2024949866
ISBN 978-1-5362-3371-1

CCP 30 29 28 27 26 25
10 9 8 7 6 5 4 3 2 1

Printed in Shenzhen, Guangdong, China

This book was typeset in Dante and Diotima Classic.

Candlewick Press
99 Dover Street
Somerville, Massachusetts 02144

www.candlewick.com

EU Authorized Representative:
HackettFlynn Ltd.,
36 Cloch Choirneal, Balrothery,
Co. Dublin, K32 C942, Ireland.
EU@walkerpublishinggroup.com

FOR MY GRAMS,
NO LONGER IN THE TIMELANDS
BUT WITH ME, ALWAYS

TRANSLATOR'S NOTE

This story has been translated from the original Seam, a language with natural measures of time: sunlight, seasons, stars.

Standardized clocks and calendars have never been in fashion.

All dialogue, unless otherwise noted, is in Seam.

All pages with kissing were translated by Fawkes.

Myriad,
WORDHOUSE TRANSLATOR

PART ONE

2

ONE

Anyone who has hiked through time knows Pocket.

It's the town travelers first reach after they stumble away from their hometime. It's the place a traveler must—with only one known exception—pass through on their way to any other when.

Once in Pocket, you simply cannot miss the temporal cobblers, where they repair the tattered soles of time boots, or the Inn of All Ways, where you can get a hot meal, a cold shower—and a reality check to expand realities. There's the wordhouse, to help with the polyglot needs of a traveler, and at the edge of town, a small shop containing a storm of fabrics and racks of precisely crafted garments from every era.

A shop called Costumes for Time Travelers.

It can be hard to put a pin in the moment a story begins. Calisto, who works at the costume shop, has a talent for pins and where to put them—and if you asked them, they would say this story began when their grandmother took out her time boots.

"What are you doing with those?" Calisto had never seen the boots out of their blue velvet shoebox, perched on the windowsill like an old pet taking a nap.

"Keep working on that ruff." Grandmother polished with industrious circles. The leather inched from dun brown to wildflower honey. "This next traveler means to leave for the Elizabethan era as soon as possible."

Calisto's worktable held a pile of unfinished ruffs, hose, and undergarments. Elizabethans needed a whole netherworld of undergarments. It took many painstaking stitches in a monstrous pair of trunk hose—puffy short pants with silk panels to be lengthened or shortened with a dramatic flourish—before they realized:

Their grandmother had not answered their question.

She was not usually slippery.

Calisto tried a direct approach. "Are you planning to put those boots *on your feet?*"

Mena—their grandmother's gifted name, short for Philomena—tucked away her polishing cloth, only to take out a tin of wax and start buffing. The boots glowed in the strong lamplight. Calisto had trimmed the wicks well, one of many thankless jobs around the shop. Some jobs they loved, others were tolerated, and a few already seemed too tedious to repeat for the rest of their life. But Mena came from a time without lightbulbs and couldn't ignore their chittering buzz or unnatural glare. And so, the lamps must be lit.

Though Pocket brought together influences from all over the timelands, Mena ran Costumes for Time Travelers like a tailor's shop in the Quattrocento. The only variations were those that allowed her to properly construct later garments, such as the gleaming sewing machines in the back. Calisto followed Mena's lead, because the costume shop was their favorite place in Pocket, and Pocket was their whole world. Something about seeing those time boots out of their box made that world wobble on its axis.

"I might lace these up again," Mena admitted.

"*When*, exactly, would you be going?" Calisto asked. Mena didn't talk about traveling, and she didn't yearn for retirement. The only time Calisto brought it up, Mena spat over both shoulders and warded herself against the evil eye.

Now she shrugged and simply said, "I might go home."

"You live behind the shop," Calisto pointed out. "You barely need to put on slippers to get here. You don't need *time boots* to get home."

Mena shook her salt-white curls. "Maybe I'm going farther."

She was a masterful tailor, but the list of things she didn't do unscrolled endlessly: leaving the shop before the lamps burned down, talking about a decision instead of doing whatever she deemed necessary, using the word *maybe*.

"Is this about your fabrics?" Calisto asked. Mena often grumbled that the swatches, yards, and bolts brought in by travelers, often by her own commission, weren't up to standards. She steamed wrinkles out of raw silk while threatening to hike into the wilds of time herself in order to hunt down quality.

"If you need something from out there"—Calisto gestured at all the time the valley was separated from—"I'll go to the Inn of All Ways and hire a traveler to bring it to our door."

"This is not a matter of fabric, I'm afraid to say."

Mena sighed. The polishing and waxing was now complete. She flipped the boots and checked the soles, which glimmered with the dark-oil rainbow sheen of all time boots. To anyone else, these would show no wear. Mena traced the smooth heel where she'd always rocked back before stepping into the mists of time. She found a hairline crack where she'd tripped while carrying eight heavy rolls of Yun brocade, its hand-shuttled silver and gold threads woven into silk, colors as soft as sunrise.

A glorious trip to China long, long before her own birth.

When Mena first acquired time boots, she'd hiked regularly. How else was she supposed to get what she needed for a tailoring business encompassing all of human history? Working cleverly with what she could carry, she'd hand-sewn and sold her wares at a stall in the all-weather market. Later, she began to dream of a sturdy and dependable shop where travelers would come to fill their needs. There had never been a costume shop like it, and Mena named three rules to guide her:

Everything correct to the era, down to the finest detail.

Everything beautiful.

Everything bespoke.

Once she had the loyalty of a fleet of travelers, she didn't need to strap on her own time boots. She could stay in her beloved shop and touch the marvelous fabrics of the timelands. She stopped traveling altogether right around the arrival of her first grandchild. Which had been a bit of a surprise, given that she'd never had any children to begin with.

Now that grandchild was staring her down with sharp grey eyes.

"It's time that I go back to when I came from," Mena admitted.

Calisto turned their stare mutely, mutinously, to a pair of Elizabethan slippers.

"You saw me tear out the seams on that churidar I was working on the other day."

"I . . . might have heard a stitch or two popping."

"I was distracted by thoughts of my hometime," Mena said. Calisto might not have believed their grandmother, except that when she blinked, her eyes unfocused, thoughts turning to *elsewhen*.

They set their work aside. "What kind of thoughts?"

Grandmother *never* talked about her hometime. Even if Calisto didn't like where this conversation had started, they were curious to see how far it would carry them into Mena's unknown past. "Everyone talks about the Rinascimento as this wonderful time for the mind. Art, science. Everything changing, everything new, but it was not so wonderful for the nose. In my little town of Chieti, I could not escape it: most things smelled vile. Pigs, eels, people using the street as a personal toilet . . ."

"*That's* how you ruined a churidar?" Calisto asked. "Thinking of your odorous hometime?"

"I did not ruin anything, and quiet. There is more. The air on the mountains was different, better than in town, brisker than Pocket. In autumn, it bore the bristle of spice. We would go out on the mountain at dawn to search for saffron in the heart of pale purple crocuses. Each flower holds delicate threads, red and gold. We picked enough tiny threads to fill great baskets. We were meant to sell this entire harvest to noble families and traveling merchants, but I always kept a pocketful to scatter into our broth. That smell means *home*."

"We can get saffron here," Calisto reminded her. "Nori uses it in her rice."

"I know this," Mena said, waving off Calisto's words with the boots.

"Do you want me to get you some?"

"It's not the same thing." The words were sharp enough, but Mena's gaze stayed glassy. "Maybe I will go back and pick crocuses again."

Calisto had never seen Mena act nostalgic. It sent them spinning toward their own strongest memories, wondering what could make them feel the same way, when they were as old as their grandmother.

A memory caught—the first time they'd run through the racks at the costume shop. They had been little, exploring with their siblings, curious about every corner of Pocket. Mena must have been busy, not able to keep an eye on the back. When they all slipped away to play a hiding game, Calisto vanished best and got lost in the forest of fabrics. They could still remember the grassy sweetness of a linen tunic, the musk of a woolen sweater, the dense spice of denim. But pigs? Eels? *Broth* that made you want to leave your calling, grandchild, and cozy town to go traipsing to the fifteenth century? If that was what nostalgia was like, people in the timelands could keep it.

"I thought you were a tailor, not a saffron hunter."

Mena shrugged. "Threads are threads."

"So that's where you learned to do . . . this?" Calisto motioned to the shop.

Mena smiled, wrinkles buckling. "I learned most of it by stealing the knowledge from my seven brothers," she said, as if those were people Calisto had *ever heard about*. "They became tailors when the art was new. I wanted to join them, but they had cruel rules about women in those days. In many, many days. So I lurked, and I taught myself. I might have stayed in the shadows of those mountains and my brothers forever, but a kind stranger told me that I was good enough to set up my own shop I started over the mountains with a pack of fabrics, buttons, patterns . . . and I ended up here."

The shop's bell rang as the door opened.

Calisto snatched their work up, pretending to be interested in the trunk hose. The traveler who walked in was the worst kind of impatient. He'd come in for measurements and spent the whole session twitching and sighing as Calisto stretched the tape over different planes of his body. Already, he was doing it again. Calisto briefly considered making his Elizabethan undergarments a size too tight—but Mena would notice.

Assuming Mena was still here.

"Calisto, why don't you head home?" Mena asked. "It's been a long night."

That was code for *there's fancy stitching I want to do all by myself.* Calisto had been helping in the shop long enough to know that there were some things Mena would never trust anyone else with, not when she had so much knowledge stored in her own hands.

What if she *did* leave? What if picking a crocus was more important than everything she'd built in Pocket? Would Calisto see Mena again? Traveling on a whim was dangerous. Calisto's mind staggered under the weight of morbid options.

"Is everything finished?" the traveler asked, tapping a toe on the floorboards. "I have something urgent in 1593."

"1593 will be there when we're done," Calisto muttered. Travelers could hike into Pocket from anywhen and hike out to *nearly* anywhen. But life in Pocket's valley moved at its own pace, and never at the frantic behest of travelers who acted like *their* trip through time was the most important one.

That was the catch about time traveling. People could start to think time belonged to them. That it made sense and would follow order. Those were the travelers who hiked into the Neolithic and never came back.

"Your pieces are nearly ready." Mena beckoned him toward the fitting room. "Whatever has worth takes time."

"Good night, Grandmother," Calisto called out.

"Good night, Calisto," she answered in a muffled tone, her mouth filled with pins.

The traveler switched from huffing to *hmmm*ing when Mena showed him the doublet. Even half-finished, her work was legendary.

Calisto couldn't imagine why their grandmother wanted to go back to a place where her talents had been untended, her brilliance held back. It made no sense. Surely Mena would see that in the morning.

Still—to be safe—Calisto stole the boots off the counter and left out the back.

TWO

Calisto opened their eyes to a small room lemony with paint and light. Clothing covered every surface and brimmed out of several trunks. Their sibling Myriad—a chosen name, Myri for short—was in her bed across the room, cocooned in sheets. This morning looked the same as most of Calisto's mornings. They would get up, head to the costume shop, and . . .

They sat up, the enormity of what they'd done breaking over them in waves.

It's one thing to make a decision rooted in a single, certain moment.

It's another to wake up with stolen time boots in your bed.

Calisto cast off the blankets. Mena's boots, nestled in the sheets, stared up, judging them. It didn't help that the laces were done up tight, crossed over the tongue in perfect *X*'s. When Calisto took the boots, they'd believed they could keep Mena in Pocket, where she belonged, where she was beloved, and possibly save her life. Now all they could think about was what would happen when Mena realized Calisto had betrayed her trust.

If they were younger, the answer might have been a few days' banishment from the costume shop. That had been the consequence when little Calisto pocketed a dozen mother-of-pearl buttons, or when a slightly older Calisto tried to finish a piece of lace point work to prove themself to Mena. Instead, they botched a stitch and ripped too many out, until what should have been a shawl was one enormous tatter.

Calisto was not quite so young. They hovered near the boundary of adulthood, wondering where it *was*. In the timelands, most eras had highly specific ideas about how and when a person crossed from one phase of life to the next, but Pocket existed outside the borders of those cultures, with no standard answers.

Why would Mena want to go back to a place where everything was dictated?

Calisto got out of bed, not wanting to wake Myri and deal with her inevitable questions about the boots. As older sibling, she'd offer advice, and Calisto couldn't bear it. They stuffed the boots into the bottom of a leather bag. Hiding the evidence didn't feel better, but at least they could walk around without drawing attention. Yes, many travelers in Pocket wore time boots, but a person carrying around someone else's was not the same. And putting them on was out of the question.

Calisto was no traveler.

Myri rolled over with a snore like a hundred zippers being pulled.

Calisto dressed, which should have been easy given the sheer volume of clothing. Some garments came from the costume shop—borrowed with Mena's permission—others were made in Pocket, purchased at the all-weather market, and many Calisto had fashioned themself. But what did someone wear to apologize to their grandmother? They had worked so hard to earn Mena's trust. Would Mena kick Calisto out of the costume shop? Before this morning, they had never even thought those words.

They couldn't unthink them now.

Calisto finished combining clothing in their unique way and double-checked the bag with the time boots. They had to get to the costume shop and apologize.

But first, they had to navigate their trio of well-meaning parents.

Richard and Tiye were in the garden.

"More eggs, please!" Nori yelled through the open kitchen window, a sizzling pan behind her voice. "I want to crack them while it's hot!"

Richard was giving a speech to the hens. They weren't laying the way they used to, and he seemed to think a lecture would help. Tiye wafted through the voluminous garden, smelling the lemon basil, plucking rosemary. She was the first to notice Calisto sneaking toward the courtyard. "What got you up with the sun?"

Calisto stopped just shy of the chicken coop. "I thought I'd . . . get back to work on that Elizabethan costume. There's still a lot to do, and the traveler is twitchy."

"If you wait, our moody hens may lay two more eggs. I can send you with enough breakfast for Mena," Nori promised as the scent of bacon slithered out the window.

"I have to keep moving," Calisto said, though they *were* tempted. Pigs didn't thrive in Pocket—they got confused by the temporal dislocation. Calisto hadn't tasted bacon's salty perfection in so long, but if they stayed, they would remain in agony-limbo. Tiye's perceptive gaze might even fall on the unmistakable outline of their bag. Or Richard might give a lecture about loyalty to the moody hens, only to uncover Calisto's theft.

And what if Calisto's siblings woke up and joined the fray?

"You have to eat something before a busy day," Nori said informatively, as though Calisto had never stopped to consider the matter of breakfast.

"I would, but . . ."

"Calisto is on an independent path," Tiye intoned, touching their shoulder. Tiye had been a priestess in an ancient civilization whose records and language were lost to later eras. Her ceremonial robe fell around her shoulders in commanding lines, scented by flowers Calisto had never been able to identify.

Richard, on the other hand, wore a three-piece suit while he gardened, and there was no mystery about it. It was one of three outfits he'd been rotating—mended by Mena—ever since he left the late twentieth century. He had taken a position as visiting history professor in Australia and got lost in Sydney Airport, arriving in Pocket with only his carry-on.

"These hens are feeling independent, making all their own choices, and sometimes that isn't a good thing," Richard said.

"Calisto is not a hen," Tiye said.

"No, they are not, but historically speaking, they—"

Tiye held up a single finger. She rang a collection of brass chimes, signifying that Richard had to obey a vow of silence, his penance for slipping into bad hometime habits.

"No starting a speech with *historically*," Nori cackled. "Quiet time until lunch!"

Richard shook his head at himself. Tiye floated over and kissed him, and he finally stopped hovering near the chickens.

Nori beckoned Calisto to the stove. She held out a curled, crisped strip of bacon. "Come on. There's plenty. A big shipment came in for the moonful festival."

"I don't deserve bacon," Calisto admitted.

They worried Nori would clamp on to that statement and shake it to see what else came out. She shook her head and wiped her greasy hands on her paprika-colored jumpsuit. As Calisto's only Pocket-born parent, she favored clothes made in the valley, brightly hand-dyed and crafted of natural fabrics including wool from the alpacas up the hill. "That's one perspective. From *my* perspective, everyone I love should have nice things."

Nori popped the bacon in Calisto's mouth. In a rush of smoky sweetness, they remembered that their family was big and boisterous but not bad—unlike the family Mena had grown up with in the timelands.

"Has Mena ever been mad at you?" Calisto asked. "And if so, what would you do to get back on her good side?"

"I would *never* cross Mena," Nori said. "Her sides are all the same." The good feeling Calisto had found melted. Nori slid the runny yolks around the pan. "I should have waited to crack these."

Tiye leaned in through the window. "Richard quieted, and the chickens blessed us." She placed an egg in each of Nori's palms and kissed her.

Nori gleefully cracked the eggs into the pan, and Calisto escaped.

Pocket was laid out like a compass, its main roads running east–west and north–south. Lesser main roads crossed from southeast to northwest and so on. Calisto lived off the southwest spoke, while the costume shop was on the east road, past the all-weather market With each step, the bag with the boots whacked their leg.

Calisto arrived at the shop around the time Mena usually opened it. She should appear with the green-tasseled keys that hung from her belt and fit them to three brass locks. Calisto waited.

Opal sunlight fell on Pocket—filtered by the mists of time all around.

It was unseasonably hot, and sweat sheeted Calisto's back as they peered inside the shop. They squinted to see beyond the display: the patterned tapestry of an uncu; an early aviator's tweed jacket and leather goggles; a fluttering yukata from the Edo period; a late survivalist high-fashion onesie with temperature-sensing fabric and knives in the hood. The lineup should have made them proud, but they couldn't see past the fear that the last few costumes they'd helped create might turn out to be their last few costumes . . . ever.

Calisto tried the door, just in case Mena had slipped in early to sew furiously. The knob clacked against their hand—locked. They had braced themself for disappointment, but Grandmother *and* her disappointments were missing.

Calisto checked the cottage behind the shop. They poked their head in the unlocked front—swept, silent, empty. The box for her time boots sat on its windowsill, the crushed velvet holding an impression like a fossil. Calisto considered putting the time boots back and pretending none of this happened, but it was too late.

Maybe Mena went out for breakfast or a walk to clear her head. Not that either of those things sounded like Mena, but they were possible. Calisto walked to the all-weather market to kill time, a phrase they'd picked up from Richard. They thought they knew what it meant, though mostly they believed that they *whiled away the time* in the costume racks, moving intuitively, searching for inspiration.

Sometimes they climbed the hills alone to watch the mists of time shift and breathe.

From a safe distance, of course.

Calisto paced through the market, past stalls, tables, and rolled-out rugs. People tried to smile, until they got a glance of Calisto's glower. They went back to the costume shop, but Mena still wasn't there. She'd never opened this late before. Was she avoiding them? Was she trying to teach some kind of torturous lesson? Or . . . had she left Pocket already?

Not possible.

Calisto checked the time boots yet again. The oily rainbow soles winked in the sunlight. Another pair of boots wouldn't be easy to come by. Travelers waited seasons to be fitted by the temporal cobblers in a slow process guided by secret formulas, but there *was* a small collection of time boots for emergency loan to trusted travelers. Like Mena.

Calisto had tried to kill time—but they had wasted it instead.

They ran all the way to the temporal cobblers. The front wall was glass. People stood outside, watching time boots being crafted, except for the pouring of soles—a process so secret, very few had witnessed it. It was easy to pick out the new traveler ensconced in a velvet fitting chair. When people found their way through the mists, their shoes were reduced to shreds. Special soles had to be engineered in order for people to stand on time, and so the art of the temporal cobbler was born.

Various styles were scattered around the shopfront on little wooden pedestals—molded calfskin Viking boots, tall Hausa riding boots, black Zao boots from the Ming dynasty, a heeled and pointy red pair for a noble of the court of Louis XIV, refurbished Doc Martens with yellow stitching around the soles. Some were highly specific while others were done in near-timeless styles, boasting a wide range of traveling options.

The workshop took up most of the space. Calisto watched a dozen cobblers swing through their duties. No Mena. They waved to their friend Adama, who stepped out of the shop to greet them. He wiped his hands on a half apron.

"Happy almost-moons, Calisto," Adama said with a wide, gapped grin.

Calisto tried to sound tuned in. "Happy almost-moons, Adama."

"What are you going to wear? Something wildly inventive, I have no doubt." Adama cocked his head. "People say the time savant might make an appearance. Though people always say that, and he's only been spotted at a few moonful festivals."

"Sure. Sorry, I need to know something. Did Mena come by and—"

"Insist on a pair of boots? I figured they were for a traveler whose costume would be ruined by their usual pair. We don't lend these out unless we know somebody down to the sole. Apologies. Cobbler's joke."

"She didn't tell you why she wanted the boots? Did she even try them on?"

Adama squinted. "She has a well-kept old pair. Why would she need another?"

Calisto held open the bag, and Adama stared into it.

He struck a hand to his chest. *"Calisto."*

"I have to stop her. She's not acting like herself."

"While I don't approve of time-boot thievery, that does sound worrisome. Mena hasn't been in the mists for a while. I would think the memory of those old traveling routes dissolves at some point, even the ones you used to tramp regularly."

"Mena did travel a lot . . . a lifetime ago. *My* lifetime, to be specific. I also don't think she *ever* went back to her hometime after she came to Pocket."

"So you should run after her, instead of worrying here with me?"

Calisto squeezed Adama's forearm and ran.

Hiking the mists of time meant memorizing directions, lest travelers get lost and end up . . . anywhen. Travelers often muttered trajectories under their breath while they got dressed at the costume shop: "Take the north road up to the mists, turn left when you enter, take twelve long steps, spin three clockwise circles, and continue on until you hit the fall of Rome." Most people picked a handful of destinations, branching out carefully. Even if Mena had found directions—travelers swapped them at the inn—she wouldn't necessarily be able to walk the route to her hometime. If Mena could become distracted enough to ruin a churidar, a garment she'd made a hundred times, she could just as easily lose the thread of her thoughts within the mists of time.

European Renaissance routes started on the west road out of Pocket. Calisto hiked upward at a bruising speed. The hills turned from gentle to punishing, just as Calisto saw her—a dot in the distance, moving toward the mist at the top. It stood like a wall, but as they drew closer, it seethed and shifted.

"Mena!" Calisto shouted, closing the distance. "Mena, wait!"

Mena turned, her face unreadable. "Oh. You." No dramatic pitch, not a single wild gesture. So she *was* mad.

"Please come back to the shop," Calisto said. "I'm sorry I took your boots, but—"

"But you know better than a woman so ancient she could be not your grandmother but your great-grandmother? A woman who has run her own shop since before your parents cut teeth? A woman who looks at Pocket's so-called elders like children in need of a nap?"

"What if something important happens while you're in the timelands?" When people traveled, it's not as if life stopped moving in Pocket.

Mena waved away this worry. "You'll tell me anything I miss."

Calisto clutched the bag to their chest. "I just want to know you'll be safe when you're going."

"I want to know that when your moment comes, you won't hide from it."

"This isn't about me," Calisto scoffed.

Grandmother gave Calisto two things: the first was her measuring look, the one she gave to silks, satins, and sables. It swept from Calisto's feet to the crown of their head, then came back down to meet their eyes.

The second was the set of keys on a green tassel from her belt.

"Really?" Calisto asked, taking it.

Grandmother sighed like a boulder shifting. "This is the deal I made with myself: if you did not return my boots, I would travel with *these*." She sat on a rock and took off the borrowed boots from the temporal cobblers. "And you would stay locked out of the shop, even if it scraped your soul." She held out her hands, and Calisto gave her the honey-colored time boots. She spoke while lacing them tight. "As you have tried to correct your mistake, you can run the shop while I'm away. Finish the work we have left. Help people dress for the moonful festival. Do not take on new travelers."

"No new travelers," Calisto agreed breathlessly. They almost couldn't believe they were getting this chance, not just to step back into the costume shop but to run it.

"You're *sure* you know the way?" they asked.

"No. But that's not the point." Mena turned to the mist like she was greeting an old friend. She rocked back on her heels, took one step—and vanished.

The cloudy wall that surrounded the valley sealed shut behind her.

THREE

Fawkes moved through the mist, toward the moons.

He'd met a million moons already. They shone down on him from all times. Leapt through their phases. It took him a long while to understand that most people saw the phases in a certain order: waxing, waning, waxing. Even longer to understand that every one he saw was the same orb, in the same sky. Fawkes's life didn't have a lot of constants.

He kept them like treasures.

His first moon shone through the boughs of ancient cedars, shattered the dark calm of branches. Not a single human glare to fight it, not a battery or a bulb.

Fawkes even knew moons he hadn't seen yet.

And one of these moonfuls in Pocket would be the night they met, though he'd no idea which one. He followed the thick stream of travelers drawn to the festival—and hurried from those who followed *him*.

.⫶⫶⫶ .⫶⫶⫶ .⫶⫶⫶

Travelers descended into the valley as the first, second, and third moons broke through above the hills. This signaled the beginning of the moonful festival—a moment when so many full moons shone in from the timelands that the night sky was terrifically illuminated.

One moon was cold silver, another ripe gold, yet another tinted coppery green. Some had hazy rings of light while others were coldly focused. Many were intent beacons; a few came shawled in darkness. As the fourth, fifth, and sixth moons arrived, the party hit its stride. Food from a dozen delicious eras was carried in and laid out on long tables. Steam rose from goat stew, curries, savory pies. Gelato from Florence was served from a cold cart that had been wheeled all the way over the hills just for the occasion.

Sights and sounds rivaled every taste. Travelers in their finest outfits—gold-threaded chakri and bell-shaped ball gowns, elegantly folded kente cloth and tsarist-era fur coats—paraded toward the Inn of All Ways. Pocket-born dancers in bright wool and bell cuffs mingled with belly dancers who shook hips covered in strings of silver coins. An artfully flailing tap troupe pounded metallic beats into a makeshift stage.

Calisto's family swirled through the well-lit chaos. Nori made the most of the moon market, where travelers laid out their finest treasures. Richard and Tiye stopped at the Inn of All Ways to catch up with old traveling friends.

Myri, along with Calisto's other siblings, wove through the crowds arm in arm. Clover—a gifted name, and the oldest—wore a pearly sheath that drank the light of the moons. Onyx—a chosen name—wore a sparkling black belt and shredded cape in the glitter-rage style. Myri wore a fringed silver dress, short as a gasp. A matching art deco headband made it look as if an entire night skyline had sprouted from her forehead.

"Happy moons, Adama!" Myri called out. The siblings located the young cobbler by the stall of a Senegalese artist and moved to meet him. He had traded in his smudged cobbler's apron for knee-length shorts and a cropped wool jacket and had lined his bare arms with painted moons in metallic shades of blue.

"What are you buying?" Myri asked.

He held out a small sculpture. "For my great-grandparents. We're celebrating their love, from leaving eighteenth-century Senegal together to becoming members of Pocket's Loose Association and Book Club of Elders. Long lifetimes are wild."

"Almost all travelers leave their hometime alone," Myri pointed out. "That's a rare love story."

Adama grinned, trying not to focus only on Myri. "You all look perfect."

"Is that a compliment for us or Calisto?" Myri asked. "You know very well they helped pick our outfits."

"Where is Calisto?" Adama asked. "Should we check the costume shop?"

"They're probably still helping people."

"Probably working too much," Onyx added.

"Just like their icon, Mena," Clover observed.

A seventh moon crested the hills with a swell of brightness.

Calisto dashed through the crowds, searching for their siblings. Leaving the shop behind, Mena-less, while knowing that people might need help with festival outfits had been harder than expected.

Dressing for the event had proven an equal challenge, but they'd found a neat solution. They'd brought their work with them, in portable fashion. Their canvas trousers were sturdy, with as many pockets as possible, stuffed full of swatches, buttons, and thread. Hanging from a wide leather belt, the green-tasseled keys to the costume shop chimed beside an arsenal of a tailor's sharpest tools. Their waistcoat combined magenta wool from Pocket with the fitted Italian construction Mena believed in like a religion—to her, *fitting* meant that the garment would not allow more than a finger's worth of room during a deep breath. As a last flourish, Calisto chose a cloak they'd constructed from many of the finest scraps gathered throughout their time at the shop. Not just a garment but wearable history.

One more detail: all the seams were on the outside.

Calisto's siblings rushed to meet them, followed by Adama.

"What did you do to your clothes?" Myri asked.

"Something I've always wanted to try but knew Mena would never go for," Calisto admitted.

"Turning yourself inside out?" Onyx said drolly.

Calisto touched the raised lines that separated one piece of fabric from another. "The seams are the most interesting part of an outfit."

Myri, Onyx, and Clover had been living with Calisto for their entire life. They no longer tried to understand them, but Clover did pinch her lips. "You look unfinished."

"I think you look exactly like yourself," Adama said.

"That's true enough." Myri laughed—not at Calisto but at Adama's sweetness.

"I say true things," Adama proclaimed. "And, Myriad, tonight you shine as strongly as anything in the skies."

Myri batted at those ridiculous words but also blushed. Adama beamed.

This situation—Adama and Myri veering from friendship to flirtation—was new. Calisto's siblings insisted that the moonful festival was the best time to find someone to kiss, but Calisto had never kissed anyone.

"Gelato?" Adama asked, pointing at the cart. "I hear they have chocolate hazelnut."

"I thought we could play spot the time savant," Myri said giddily.

With Mena's time boots returned, Calisto jarringly remembered that Adama had also mentioned the time savant earlier. Apparently it was all the rage in the timelands to gawk at differences for sport, but Pocket had been founded by travelers who walked away from that, toward a life outside of a need for *normal*. Here they could be together and unique.

"Why are you spotting him?" Calisto asked. "It's one thing to be curious about unique abilities. It's another to turn a person into a sideshow for festival entertainment."

"We're not turning him into anything. He's not going to show," Onyx cleared up. "How many moonful festivals has he bothered to make an appearance at? Two? Three?"

Calisto shrugged. They'd never gotten a glimpse of him.

"He doesn't use Pocket as a way station like everyone else," Adama said. "He just kicks around from one period to the next. No valley in between."

"That is categorically impossible," Clover stated. "Why doesn't he get lost in the mists, if he's traveling without directions?"

"All the more reason to find him, so I can ask!" Myri said. "If he ever does grace us with his mysterious presence, I am going to interview him for the wordhouse. There are some odd things said about him, but no one has ever *asked him.*"

"Exactly," Onyx intoned. "I'd like to know why people say he's going to bring about the end of time."

"Or if he already caused an apocalypse and is hiding from it," Clover added.

"I heard he can fly," Adama said, which stopped everyone. "What? I did."

"He's not a wizard or a superhero. He's a time traveler," Myri reminded Adama. "Come on, let's get a better view from over there. Oh! Rare books!"

Calisto's siblings headed toward the carts. They were apprentices at the wordhouse, and their voracious appetites for language knew no bounds. Myri picked through a cart of some of the timelands' earliest novels, in the original Japanese. She hoped to be a translator from timelands' tongues into Seam. Calisto was the only one who knew the other half of her dream: translating stories from Seam and ferrying them *out* to the timelands.

Clover and Onyx competed to see who could snag the most depressing Russian literature. They were both training to don the shared time boots of the wordhouse and assist travelers on long trips to avoid the perils of cultural miscommunication. Neither had gone on any translation trips yet—but Clover had done immersion travel. Nobody believes they know more about the world than a sibling who has returned from a century abroad. Every time Calisto picked up a book, Clover leaned close and wrinkled her nose. "Not worth it." Or "Ugh, awful translation." Or "Can you *still* only read two languages besides Seam?"

"I know words for garments and stitches and fabrics in a hundred languages," Calisto said. "Also, fashion *is* a language."

"What is this saying?" Myri asked, picking at Calisto's many-scrap cloak.

Calisto snatched it away. "That defies simple translation."

Onyx snorted. "It makes you look like a monster from a fairy tale."

"I don't mind," Calisto said. "Monsters are always the best dressed."

"You mean villains," Clover said. "*Villains* are the best dressed in fairy tales."

"Oooh." Myri raised one purposeful finger. "Let's check out the fairy tale cart."

Calisto's siblings paid for their books with moon coins, and Adama set off toward the gelato with a determined look. Calisto drifted toward the center of the market. The moons were strong, washing almost everything with light, but a few spots were left to the dark. Those shadows felt a little *too* dark, too deep, too much like doubled folds where anything might be tucked away.

Calisto told themself to stop being silly and enjoy the festival. They tried to bask in the glorious spread of costumes and take note of greetings that came their way. They were attending as the tailor of Pocket for the first time, though that also meant Mena *wasn't* there for the first time. Of course, she had always refused to leave the shop and celebrate, but having her nearby had been Calisto's constant.

It wasn't only Mena's absence that prickled at Calisto.

There was a *presence* in those shadows.

A strong crosswind halted Calisto's thoughts. Their cloak rippled, then nearly ripped off. They looked to the Inn of All

Ways the great chimera of a building at the heart of Pocket, the architecture of a hundred eras smashed together. It was a place of mismatched doors and windows, with beds of pallet straw, chestnut four-posters, memory foam, hammocks, and so forth. The highest tower held a great brass bell. Atop the gabled, thatched, marbled, and chimney-strewn roof, iron weather vanes took the measure of Pocket's winds. They were screeching in wild circles.

High above, Calisto noticed a scrap of darkness in the sky. "What is that?" they asked, calling out to their siblings. The scrap twisted—a slender figure caught against the backdrop of the night. "*Who* is that?"

"Look!" Myri shouted. "Calisto actually spotted the time savant!"

"The time savant?" The words came from every direction, echoed in languages and textured with tones. Fearful, reverent, thrilled.

All seven moons seemed like stage lighting, pointing. The time savant fell like a leaf. He spun above the Inn of All Ways, narrowly missing impalement on one of the pointiest weather vanes.

Adama materialized, swallowing a last bite of gelato. "Told you he could fly."

"Is that what you call . . . that?" Calisto asked as the figure pin-wheeled over the town.

While other travelers hiked from the hills in a careful and methodical fashion, the time savant crashed into Pocket in slow motion. He was an acrobat shrugging off the laws of physics. Elegantly wild, or wildly elegant. He landed in a heap of dark-rainbow soles and shredded clothes in front of the Inn of All Ways. During a silent review from the crowd, he stood, dusted his pants, and gave a self-conscious little bow.

"*The time savant!*" so many people cheered that Calisto felt furious on his behalf.

His clothes were so ruined that Calisto surged toward him, grateful for the arsenal in their pockets. Mouth full of pins, they went to work. The crowd was still celebrating his appearance. "What's your name?" they asked.

He blinked, struck.

Fawkes looked at Calisto and saw *everything*.

"Calisto," he said, breathless in the wake of all their time together.

"That's me." They glanced up. "Did my reputation as a tailor precede me?"

Calisto *did* precede themself, but not in the way they meant. Fawkes's mind gave him shards of his life to sift through. Moments without order. He'd glimpsed Calisto many times. Dreamed their name. Truly, Fawkes didn't know how to answer this question in a way that would help anyone else understand. The only answer he knew was: "Calisto."

A constant, bright as the moon.

"That's . . . still me." Calisto bridged a few gaping holes with safety pins.

Everyone was watching. The time savant's spotlight was big enough for two, but Calisto wasn't sure they wanted to be in it. They shifted backward, and he finally said:

"Fawkes. My name is Fawkes."

He felt the shadow in the crowd, the threat he'd run from since he was small.

Usually they didn't get this close.

Fawkes threw his arms around Calisto. They held on, confused. This embrace knew the exact dimensions and angles between them. There was something dizzyingly *not-strange* about having this stranger so close. He smelled like an electrical storm, and long, hard walks, and worn leather.

"Let's go," he whispered in Calisto's ear, "before the rest catch up."

FOUR

Calisto took Fawkes to the costume shop for three distinct reasons.

First: taking him home could prove disastrous. Everyone was enjoying the moonful festival, but eventually the night would end. If the time savant—*Fawkes*—was in the kitchen, the heady combination of siblings and parents could send him running. He was skittish. Calisto felt like he could vanish as quickly as he'd blown into town.

Second: whatever Fawkes called *the rest* did not sound good.

Third: his clothes were a catastrophe. He'd wrecked them so thoroughly that it was hard to tell how they'd originated. Calisto's fingers itched to set it all on fire and start again.

They led Fawkes down the east road. A few of the nosiest people were attuned to the time savant, but most had been drawn back into the festival. They probably thought Fawkes's arrival was a performance, like the dancers who were launching into a new number, pulling people from the crowd to join. Calisto caught a glimpse of Myri and Adama spinning each other.

As they left behind the music and smells, Calisto found themself alone with Fawkes. He alternated between dodging shadows and casting desperate looks over his shoulders, double-checking each patch of darkness.

Calisto fumbled Mena's keys. It was hard to match each tiny, toothy slice to the correct lock.

"Hurry," Fawkes said, reaching for the knob.

Calisto finished unlatching the first lock, then had to start over to find the second key. They didn't feel like they were offering much, in terms of rescues. "Do you . . . make entrances like that in the timelands, too? Or is Pocket special?" Calisto often distracted Mena with chatter, but they were scraping for things to say. If they could help Fawkes look less frightened, maybe they could keep themself from panicking. "I like your name. Fawkes. Was it gifted or chosen?"

He didn't answer. Maybe they didn't use those terms when he was from. Calisto didn't know much about him—only the rumors, which were entirely suspect.

"Did you pick your name?" Calisto tried again.

"The grown-up gave it to me."

The grown-up. Well, that was an interesting way to put it. "Do you only know one grown-up? I know so many. An abundance of grown-ups. An embarrassment of grown-ups. I think that should be the group term, in fact. I have siblings who work at the word-house—I should see about making it official."

The second lock let go with a click. Caught up in triumph, Calisto dropped the keys.

"So you know my name. Somehow. Do you want to guess who

gifted it to me?" They didn't wait for an answer. "An oracle. Which is not quite as dramatic as it sounds. You see, my parents   "

"Hurry, please."

Calisto had tried two of the keys in the third lock and been wrong both times. They snatched up what *had* to be the right one. "Who are you afraid of?" they asked, remembering that feeling in the crowd—the doubled-over darkness, the hovering fear.

"They call themselves Time Wardens," Fawkes said.

Cold skittered under Calisto's cloak and up the back of their arms.

The third lock gave way, and the door swung open. As soon as they were both inside, Fawkes sealed the door, throwing bolts with the intensity of lightning striking ground.

The fear leached out of him, replaced by a deep exhaustion. It seemed that Fawkes had decided that this level of safety, whatever it was, would have to do. He turned in a weary circle and faced the costume shop, not seeming to take it in whatsoever.

The shop was different in the dark, without Mena. Even when they both stayed late working, Mena hummed and hurried about in the lamplight. Now seven moons cut through the front windows and reached long, cold fingers, picking through the silent racks.

With a great groan, Fawkes hoisted himself onto Calisto's cutting table and set himself down cross-legged right where they usually worked.

Calisto took that as an invitation.

They fished out their best measuring tape and turned around him, not touching without his permission, but snapping the tape over the various lines of his body.

Fawkes's eyes were unfocused, and not in the usual way. When

Calisto got a look at them, they seemed to match the mists of time at the top of the hill. Opaque, yet swirling. Fawkes didn't notice Calisto whipping the tape in circles around his neck and waist.

They scribbled a few numbers as he napped . . . sitting up? "I need to know when you're going next so I can work on a costume." The offer slipped out so naturally that they didn't have a chance to think it all the way through.

No new travelers.

They'd promised Mena. They couldn't end their first night in charge by tossing out her only rule. "I can't make a *whole* costume right now. It's a long story with a strict grandmother. I'll just have to patch up . . . whatever you're wearing."

Now that he sat in front of them—there, and yet not present— Calisto had the perfect excuse to study his clothes. Besides their general state of ruin, everything hung three sizes too large. Calisto could make out individual pieces: a washed black denim trucker jacket worn to a whisper. A billowing cream shirt with a high collar and elaborate cuffs over a duct-tape undershirt. Pants with thermal sensors that had been hacked into shorts and probably started out eggplant in color. Thick wool socks. And black leather steel-toed time boots with yellow laces and those distinctive iridescent soles.

His boots were the most worn-out pair Calisto had ever seen, but at least they felt *familiar*. The rest of his clothes added up not to an answer but to a riddle. The jacket had to be from the twentieth century. The shirt was Jacobean. Those pants were made from fashion tech manufactured right before the Industrial Collapse. And then there was the undershirt, which seemed to hail from an even later date. Calisto had only seen a few garments like it before, on travelers who got close to the last known moments in the timelands, when the only thing to do was patch together what you could with what was left: duct tape, safety pins, emergency sewing kits. Some people called it postpocalypse. Or endpunk.

Calisto recalled the rumor that the time savant had caused the catastrophe that stopped every other traveler short—the mysterious *something* that kept anyone from hiking past a certain point. Calisto didn't believe that Fawkes was a time-booted harbinger of doom. And yet.

There was something strange and desperate about his attire.

"How long have you been wearing that outfit?" Calisto asked.

Fawkes shook his head, the mists in his eyes draining off. They shifted to a solid color that didn't bear any resemblance to the previous clouds: dark brown, filigreed with gold.

Calisto repeated the question. "How long have you been wearing these clothes, in this particular arrangement?"

Fawkes shrugged. "I grew out of my last outfit a while ago. When I got taller."

Calisto set aside the tape measure. "Are you telling me that you've been all over the timelands wearing *this* set of clothes and lived to make cryptic statements about it?"

Fawkes nodded.

Calisto let out a dusky, nervous laugh. Even though Fawkes was sitting in front of them, unharmed—at least on the surface—it was retroactively terrifying to think about moving through eras without the protective coloration of a costume. Mena had taught them that the right costume could be a matter of survival, as well as a thing of beauty. "I can't send you back into the timelands like that. For multiple reasons. Why don't you stay in Pocket until my grandmother gets back? This is her shop. She made me promise—"

"That you won't make costumes for new travelers."

"How did you guess that?"

"Oh." Fawkes reached into the drawer below where he was sitting. "You keep snacks in your cutting table." He found a bag of spiced nuts that Calisto had been saving and swallowed half of them in one go.

"How do you know that? And how do you know what my grandmother made me promise?" Calisto was more fascinated than frustrated with Fawkes, but the line between the two was growing thin. "It's time for you to explain."

Fawkes seemed to do some kind of inner calculation. "All right. But you can't blame me for what you learn."

"Fair enough."

Fawkes finished off the bag of nuts. Quiet thickened. "What if I said we know each other? Not *already*, because *already* implies past. What if I said that we do? You will ask a hundred questions. And I might reveal that I see my life out of order. And you'll put pins in your mouth and make yourself busy while you puzzle what I mean, which I've seen you do many times. Not from my childhood, from what I've seen will come."

Calisto caught themself against the table with a hand, unbalanced. "I'm not a stranger to you," they said. "But you're a stranger to me. We met for the first time tonight . . . linearly speaking."

It should have thrown them off completely.

And yet.

They'd grown up in Pocket, where the dance of time had different steps. They knew how important it was to keep an open mind. This would explain why Fawkes looked at Calisto like they'd known each other for ages. It would put some context to why a young traveler who'd been hiking through the timelands alone for so long trusted them on first sight—for him, it wasn't *first sight* at all.

Fawkes looked down at the tread of his boots as if the mysteries of the universe had gotten caught there. "You look at me like you *don't* know me, and that feels confusing."

Calisto fought the desire to pile on questions, exactly as Fawkes had predicted. They did, however, slide a pin in one side of their mouth. It helped them think.

"You know . . ." New understanding broke through. "This is good news for us, Fawkes."

"It is?"

"You say you know me—"

"Because I do," Fawkes broke in earnestly.

"Have I ever made or given you something to wear?" Calisto prompted.

"Of course." He smiled at the memory of something that hadn't happened yet—which gave Calisto a touch of vertigo.

"Then you're not a new traveler. I'm not breaking Grandmother's rule." Calisto felt the oddities of spacetime wrap around their hopes. "I can make you a costume."

FIVE

The moonful festival had let loose a cascade of moments—moments that Fawkes was wading through when he woke at first light. He hadn't felt so unmoored since he left his hometime: a dark, unmapped era. The sun murderously hot, the great trees strong enough to ward off the rays and keep him safe. He'd spent most of his early life sticking close to the place where he was born.

Even before time boots, his mind moved in its own way.

That's how Fawkes found Calisto. A rush of pale brown hair. A mouthful of bright pins. A steady presence at his side. That was all Fawkes knew until he got older—and a pair of black boots with every-color-kissed soles came into his life. As he traveled, he chased flashes of what he and Calisto could become, but the beginning, middle, and end were all tangled inside.

When Calisto returned the next morning, they pulled back the curtain of heavy fabric that Fawkes had draped over the cutting table so he could curl up and sleep beneath it.

"Are you sure you're okay down there?"

"I can sleep anywhere," Fawkes said. It was one of his best abilities as a traveler who didn't always have the loveliest options. Calisto had food. Tea. Hot, black, spiced with cloves. And dumplings. Thick, chewy, singing with salt. A ravenous feeling twisted through Fawkes. He'd been hungry for so long.

Calisto looked at him with that bright, ready gaze, and Fawkes knew what it meant.

"Let's find you something to wear."

The racks swallowed them both.

Fawkes hadn't imagined there could be so many clothes, all special. He'd hiked through times when there was less, and times when there was more, but *more* didn't usually mean *better*. He'd hiked through royal palaces and courtyards crusted with jewels and slathered in gold, only to find people starving on the other side of the walls. He'd hiked to post-post-industrial eras and slept in the skeletons of mammoth chain stores.

Pocket was different. No wonder Calisto loved it with such a ferocity. No wonder there were people who would hurt it so easily.

"What do you like?" Calisto asked, jarring him present. This moment, with them, in the costume shop. It felt small but important. They'd bent their grandmother's rules to let him be part of their life. They'd acted like it wasn't bending, but it was.

"What I'm wearing is fine," Fawkes said. The shirt had holes, but the fabric and his skin were so familiar. He didn't know how long it would take to wear in a new outfit.

"We're not aiming for *fine*," Calisto said. "If you're going to live in what I give you, it has to be spectacular."

Fawkes was already a spectacle to Pocket. He wouldn't mind being *less* spectacular.

"When are you headed?" Calisto asked.

"Impossible to say."

"I know you might not have picked a destination yet, but—"

"I don't. I can't. Hike anywhere or anywhen on purpose."

"You could, though, couldn't you? Other travelers follow directions if they want to make it to the timelands."

"I get to the timelands easily enough, I just can't control when I land." Fawkes paused, working something out. "Some first traveler had to figure out those directions in the first place, didn't they?"

"Yes, but that was generations ago. And dangerous. Now travelers can build on known routes."

"When I try to follow someone else's directions . . ." His fingers flitted around, a hopeless scattering. Traveling that way had never felt right to Fawkes, even before it conclusively failed and he ended up at the Salem witch trials instead of a Victorian séance.

"How did you get *here*, then?"

Fawkes shrugged. "I saw all the travelers headed this way for the festival."

"So you don't have to travel through Pocket, but your trips are entirely arbitrary?" Calisto puffed a sigh. "Let's go back to costume basics. Colors? Styles? Fits?" they rattled off. "Any direction you can give me, whatsoever?"

Fawkes didn't answer at first. He had gotten pulled in by a jacket of viridian green velvet. It *felt* like something he knew. Like the loosely woven blanket of cedar branches overhead closing in, keeping him safe. "This?"

Calisto shook their head. "This is going to take so much more work than I thought."

The shop's bell rang out.

"I'll be right back," Calisto said, rushing toward the front.

A traveler was already inside, waiting. "I leave for the Elizabethan era at once, and I've heard that Philomena isn't even here. Are *you* able to finish this costume?"

"I am," Calisto said, voice frosted like the ice age Fawkes had accidentally wandered into. He'd nearly lost several toes hiking back out.

"Fine," the traveler said. "Are you ready to fit the doublet? Because—"

"I said I'm *able* to finish the job, not that I'll drop everything to do it. We're closed the day after the moonful festival."

"That's not true. Since when?"

Fawkes edged out in the aisle until he could see the man's face, flaring red. Calisto ushered the traveler out, waving him away.

"How long will you be closed?" he asked.

"Until I open the door." Calisto slammed it behind the traveler and threw the bolts home. "Come back later!"

"I'm never coming back to this horrible shop!" the traveler shouted.

Fawkes emerged from the racks. "Will that cause another problem?"

Calisto shrugged. "I don't care."

They worked in the shop without any more interruptions, Calisto measuring, cutting, stitching. Fawkes watched them in wonder. Nobody had ever reordered their world for him, not even the littlest bit.

/// /// ///

That night, Calisto left Fawkes asleep under Mena's cutting table again.

Their mind was humming from work, their fingertips dead to the world. They crossed the market, still scattered with the remnants of the moonful festival—glittering streamers on the lampposts, painted moons hanging from the trees.

Pocket was quiet, and it lulled Calisto toward their bed.

So, of course, their entire family was downstairs when they got home. Myri and Onyx were reading, Nori and Tiye were sitting nearly on top of each other and going over plans for the garden, Richard and Clover were playing a stalemated game of chess. Nobody was waiting up for Calisto, but everyone was ready to pounce the moment they walked in the door.

"Where have you been all day?" Myri put a finger in her book to mark the place. "Is there that much work at the shop? The festival is over. The town is nearly empty."

"Be careful doing inventory," Nori said with one eye on a sketch of the proposed vegetable patch. "Mena won't like it if you move things around too much."

Calisto was certainly rearranging things. Since Fawkes's arrival, they had been too busy to worry that Mena might disapprove—but Calisto found they were willing to risk it. Mena had risked more just to go back to her hometime and literally smell the flowers.

When she returned, would Mena be impressed with the work they were doing for Fawkes? Would Calisto reveal what he said about the connection they had?

Would Calisto tell *anyone* about that?

As if tapping into their thoughts, Clover eyed them over the chessboard. "Still thinking about the time savant?"

43

"He was so *strange* and *abrupt* with you at the festival," Myri marveled.

"But I think that's . . . him?" Onyx offered.

Calisto held in a laugh at the idea that Onyx—or any of their siblings—knew the time savant better than they did.

Even so, Fawkes knew far more about Calisto than they did about him.

"How long did he stay after you took him to the costume shop?" Myri asked. "Did you get a hint of where he's going?"

Calisto could tell that Myri's curiosity had been gnawing at her since last night. The whole family watched eagerly. Calisto shrugged. They couldn't tell anyone, not even their family, about helping Fawkes. Not until he was safely out of Pocket. Even if his fears of being followed were unfounded, Calisto didn't want their talkative family to be the reason someone caught him.

"Have you ever heard of the Time Wardens?" Calisto asked.

Nori stared too hard at the paper. "Why do you ask?"

"Just something the time savant said. Before he vanished." That was true—he'd gone somewhere in his mind, without leaving the costume shop.

"He's slippery," Myri said, and returned to her book as if that concluded everything.

"There's cauliflower stew on the stove," Richard added.

"I need a bed," Calisto admitted, not just to Richard but also in response to Fawkes sleeping so soundly on the shop floor. Their body ached with all the work they'd done. It wasn't a bad sensation. It made them feel like a real tailor, even more than Mena handing over the keys to the shop. And there was another long day of work ahead.

44

"I might sleep at Mena's cottage until she comes back," they called down as they stiffly climbed the stairs.

"Don't spend *too* much time alone," Nori called up.

"Costumes don't count!" Clover added.

"I won't," Calisto quietly promised as they reached the landing.

Fawkes and Calisto sat together in the wreckage of another dumpling breakfast. Calisto sipped at the overbrewed remains of their cold tea as they put the finishing touches on a stack of garments.

"You can't *hover*," they said, waving him away with brushstrokes of their hand.

"What else should I do?" Fawkes asked.

"Go contemplate your next steps."

Fawkes paced over to the fitting rooms. Paced back. And then, without any warning, he went to that misty place. His eyes filled with thick, swirling clouds. Calisto worried that he would hit the floor, unable to hold himself up while his consciousness was elsewhere—or elsewhen. But he kept walking, his steps slower, dreamier.

Then he shook it off with a few jerks of his head.

"Huh," he said. "I'm going to a play."

"That's nice," Calisto mumbled through a mouthful of pins. "We have plays in Pocket. I just saw a group of travelers put on a Bunraku puppet show. Before that, it was a Fosse musical and a Spanish golden age drama. I've seen theater from all over the centuries. I like most of it. The Greek tragedies are a lot of wailing."

Fawkes ran over to Calisto. "I mean, that's where I'm hiking next. The opening of one of Shakespeare's plays."

"I thought you can't hike anywhere or anywhen on purpose!"

45

Calisto threw their hands up, dangerously close to taking on Mena's wild gestures in her absence.

"I can't. But sometimes I *do* see bits of what I'll do, a hint to where the present is going to spit me out."

Calisto aligned this information with how it felt to watch him disappear, even though his body stayed. They believed in his mind-travel, but they still had to ask: "Are you *sure* that's when you're going next? Because if it is, I have to start a whole new costume."

Fawkes evaded the question. "It's going to be the one with the mean fairies, and the people who run in the woods squirting magic flower juice on each other."

"*A Midsummer Night's Dream?*" Calisto asked, faintly recognizing the play through the haze of Fawkes's description.

"Yes!"

"It had to be Elizabethan," Calisto muttered. If they set aside the era's cursedly difficult costumes and complicated sumptuary laws—which happily condemned a person for wearing the wrong breeches—Calisto loved Shakespeare. They had seen all of his plays, including a few lost to the later canon, in the grassy field north of the market, when the blue dusk lingered, and the whole valley hushed for words that echoed across ages.

Calisto was hardly the only one to love Shakespeare. On any given night at the Globe Theatre, a few dozen members of the audience might be travelers.

"Will you be all right in that era? Do you speak English?" For someone who didn't come through Pocket often, Fawkes knew Seam well. Most travelers spoke more than one language, but there were so many out there in the timelands. "We could get you someone from the wordhouse to go with—"

"No need." Fawkes switched over without hesitation. "English isn't a pretty one, but Shakespeare makes it interesting."

"What's your first language?"

"I don't know," Fawkes said. "They get mixed up in my early memories."

"I only have English and Italian, besides Seam," Calisto admitted. They'd learned English from Richard, or rather from the books he collected. Italian was a gift from Mena, who also spoke a dialect and used the elaborate hand gestures she called a language in their own right.

"What other languages do you speak?" Calisto asked.

Fawkes launched into a bright stream of Arabic, followed by an early form of German, a bit of Hindi, and then an equally lilting language that sounded like . . . Welsh? Fawkes kept swapping out languages, midsentence. Dozens of them.

Calisto wondered if he had any idea how rare this ability was. They'd watched Myri and Onyx and Clover—all bright and motivated—add one new language at a time to their expanding stores of knowledge. None of them could do anything like this.

"Do people from your hometime pick up languages like that?" Calisto asked.

"What people?" Fawkes asked.

Calisto startled. Something about stumbling into Fawkes's past felt like blinking and finding yourself at the bottom of a deep pit. "*When* are you from, Fawkes?"

He looked bewildered, held under the surface of bad memories.

"*Where* are you from?" Calisto tried instead.

The grimace on Fawkes's face thawed. "The great cedars. I found them in other times. Some of those eras are called Phoenicia. There's a later one called Lebanon."

"From what I've learned about the timelands, Phoenicia is a civilization and Lebanon is a country," Calisto said. "Why are you calling them eras?"

"People think about *place* backward. A country has a location, but land is a place. A town, civilization, kingdom, or country always changes. The place remains. The name and borders fade like ideas."

"Hmmm." Calisto took a seam ripper to the green velvet jacket.

"Are you really going to start all over?" Fawkes asked.

They kept ripping. "Yes and no."

Fawkes wasn't the only one who could be mysterious.

Calisto had made not one costume, but three.

They gathered everything up into piles and put one in each of the costume shop's fitting rooms.

"Why are there so many?" Fawkes asked. He riffled through the pile in the first fitting room. "Are there different sets of clothes to go *under* the clothes?"

"This isn't new information," Calisto argued. Fawkes was enjoying the softest terry cloth robe in the shop, and beneath it he wore his own flimsy boxers and a ragged chest binding. They'd provided fresh options for each of the costumes.

Fawkes unfolded everything in the first fitting room. "I didn't realize there could be so *many* underclothes. Do they all have their own names? What is this one called?" he asked, waving around a white square. Calisto attempted to imagine what Mena would do under these trying circumstances and came up blank.

"Let's go back to the larger question: Why so many clothes? Because you travel without coming to Pocket, and you don't always know when you're going to land. It's my job to make sure you can safely move through as many eras as possible." And with that, Calisto shut the door of the fitting room.

Fawkes emerged in loose brown trousers in the shalwar style, a white under-tunic that skimmed his torso, and a green-and-yellow-striped over-tunic of linen. Calisto had based this choice on Fawkes's homeplace—if not his hometime—among the great cedars. These garments could be found over swaths of centuries, with slight variations. He could travel widely in them without major alterations. And because he wouldn't take off his boots for anything—including sleep—they'd fashioned a covering out of hand-dyed leather.

Fawkes closed one eye and looked at Calisto. "Is this right?"

"A draped garment is hard to mess up," Calisto said.

Fawkes had a stunning lack of reaction. He spun into the second fitting room. There was so much thumping that Calisto almost offered to help but stopped themself.

Let Fawkes fumble. Even the concept of seeing him in the middle of a costume change was turning them bright red.

Their cheeks were still pink when Fawkes came out. Here was the outfit Calisto had chosen for the later eras in the timelands, the Enlightenment through the Industrial Collapse. Fortunately, fashion offered a garment that didn't change much: the three-piece suit. Calisto had picked a dark shade of moss—Fawkes looked good in greens—and done the trousers, vest, and single-breasted jacket in the lightest wool, using a proper floating canvas, even though Fawkes would never know the difference. He had failed to figure out the black silk tie. He was wearing it flung over one shoulder like a scarf.

Calisto could fix that.

They rushed over, pulling the tie into a neat half Windsor.

"Watch my fingers." Fawkes looked down as Calisto knotted. When he looked up again, Calisto felt like their face was being memorized. Or remembered.

Or both at the same time.

Right as the moment found its natural peak of awkwardness, Fawkes broke away. "I like the way this feels." He ran his palms down the trousers. "It's soft."

Calisto felt hesitation lurking somewhere in the compliment. "But?"

"I've seen a lot of these. As a traveler. They seem like they are for other people."

"Rich people?" Calisto guessed.

"Old people."

Calisto's curiosity flared like a match. "Everyone talks like you've been traveling for a long time, but you don't seem older than I am. When did you start?"

"My teeth were half out." Fawkes held out his hand at waist height. "What's this old?"

Calisto murmured. "No wonder people call you a savant." New travelers were in the proximity of adulthood, or full adults, by timelands measures. Fawkes had started much earlier. It was impressive on one hand, but on the other, Calisto couldn't imagine what it would feel like to live that way, moving through eras as a child, turned around by each set of rules, especially without a place like Pocket as a safe harbor.

Calisto had grown up outside of time, and Fawkes had grown up *all over* time.

"All right," Calisto said. "Last costume. The Elizabethan one."

Fawkes tucked himself into the final fitting room.

50

He came out a third time, looking resplendent and uncomfort able. He wore a pair of beribboned hose with Venetians—puffed breeches that fell at the knee—a doublet with slashed sleeves made from the viridian velvet jacket, a flowing white shirt, and a fur-lined damask robe. These were some of the best and most obnoxiously complicated pieces Calisto had ever made, and Fawkes was slouching in them like they were questionable pajamas.

"These shorts feel like marshmallows." Fawkes poked at them.

"They're breeches," Calisto said. "And you look perfect."

Everything was how Mena would have done it, according to the strict letter of the era. But Fawkes looked miserable. It was hardly the reaction Calisto had hoped for.

"One more thing."

Calisto rushed to the back room and returned with a canvas drawstring pack to hold the costumes. In the bottom, they'd tucked what was left of Fawkes's old clothes, washed in Mena's lavender soap and folded gently. "I left those for sentimental value *only*." Fawkes put his face to the ruined fabric and nuzzled it.

He tucked the rest of the costumes inside and slung the pack over his shoulder.

"You're leaving?" Calisto asked, instantly adrift. They'd grown used to Fawkes's presence with a stunning swiftness.

"It's safer if I go as soon as possible. I'm going to pay, of course."

"Even if you don't have our coins, I trust you to pay." The moon coins traded at the market—fulls, halves, and crescents—stood for the currency of Pocket: time. Each was a pledge to give a certain amount, in whatever way was agreed on by both parties.

Fawkes smiled, and it was dazzling, and Calisto remembered that he'd literally flown into Pocket on a rogue wind. They'd gotten comfortable with him, but he was wild. "I have something specific in mind."

With that, he turned on the heel of one boot and was gone.

Darkness had fallen. Calisto blew out the lamps. They meant to make it to Mena's cottage to sleep, but they were so tired. Without thinking, they melted to the floor, beneath Mena's cutting table, pulled the curtain Fawkes had rigged, and fell asleep.

When they stirred again, the sun was high. They had been dreaming about a thunderstorm. It had rattled all the way down to their bones. A few last, loud *claps* detached them from the dream. Calisto sat up in the enclosed calm under Mena's cutting table.

Next to them was a pair of time boots. They were reddish brown, and despite looking sturdy, they were deeply worn, the stitching and laces caked in dust. This was not a brand-new pair from the temporal cobblers, or even a borrowed pair like the ones Mena had almost marched out of Pocket with. The dark-rainbow soles held a crust of mud.

This was how Fawkes was paying them back? With dirty, mysterious time boots they would never wear?

But that wasn't the only surprise waiting.

Calisto pulled aside the curtain. The costume shop had been ransacked.

SIX

Calisto had broken Mena's only rule.

They'd made costumes for a new traveler—no matter the time-warping logic they'd used to get around the truth. Fawkes *was* a new traveler to the shop, one with people after him, which had seemed like a faraway threat until it was right on their doorstep. Calisto had fallen asleep under the cutting table with the door unlocked. They might as well have left it wide open with a note that said *Ruin whatever you like as long as you don't wake me up.*

Now they understood what *had* woken them. It wasn't dream-thunder at all but the pounding of boots. They flew out of the shop and into the street, turning around in a circle. In the distance, a group of people was literally heading for the hills. They moved at a high march. Calisto got one glimpse of who had done this before they disappeared into the mists. Something about their outfits caught Calisto's eye and taunted their brain.

Uniforms.

They were wearing uniforms, like you might expect from an army brigade or a police squadron in the timelands. But unlike those groups, they were all wearing *different* uniforms—with weapons to match. Olive-green drab with guns, dark blue wool with bully sticks, chain mail and glinting swords. The only thing they had in common were time boots, highly polished.

Calisto locked the door of the shop—far too late.

And went in search of answers.

Calisto expected Nori to hem and haw, to offer Calisto breakfast, to ask a hundred questions. Instead, her legs gave out, and she sat down on the doorstep.

"That sounds like Time Wardens."

"I tried to ask you about them!" Calisto exclaimed. "Who are these travelers?"

What do they want with Fawkes?

"They're not natural travelers. They steal time boots." Nori was still clutching a giant pair of garden shears, wearing a floppy sun hat. Something about the serious topic and the silly outfit made the whole thing more urgent. "They want to go back to a time before travelers, when no one had boots or knew paths through the mists. According to Time Wardens, travelers will inevitably upset the 'one true timeline,' as they call it. They believe it's their job to protect the known order of things . . . no matter how awful that order happens to be. Most of them came from groups in the timelands who believed the same thing. Militaries, police forces, groups dedicated to order through force."

"That explains the costumes," Calisto muttered.

Nori put the shears down. "They single out anyone who moves

through the mists differently. Pairs, people on particularly long hikes, anyone who sticks out." Fawkes fit several elements of that description. "Or who they think might change the existing flow of time. It's bad news for travelers when wardens show their . . . well, their faces are not exactly faces in the traditional sense."

Calisto had only seen their backs retreating into the mists, but Fawkes had brought this up in his own way, the night they met. "They're *faceless*?"

"They have features . . . eyes and noses and all the rest. It's just that nobody can seem to remember what they look like after seeing them. Time Wardens wait in the mists, the better to regulate everyone's travel. Nobody is meant to live behind the curtains of time like that. It . . . warps them."

"Why have I never heard about *any* of this?" Calisto asked. The lack of information was starting to feel like a grand and unwelcome pattern—first Mena's past, then Fawkes's foreknowledge, and now a threat that had been lurking around Pocket this whole time without Calisto knowing.

"It's been a long time since anyone came back to Pocket and reported a sighting. We thought they might be gone, dispersed. Apparently they were just—"

"Biding their time?"

Nori nodded. "Maybe they were keeping an eye on the costume shop and noticed that Mena left. Do you think they were trying to steal something?"

Or someone, Calisto narrowly avoided saying.

Fawkes had left Pocket. Why was Calisto still keeping him like a secret? And why were they carrying around the time boots he'd left behind, in the same bag that they'd been using for Mena's? They were even *less* likely to wear these with Time Wardens in the picture, and it hadn't been very likely to begin with.

"My parents . . ." Nori said. "They taught me to fear the Time Wardens." Calisto couldn't remember Nori's parents being afraid of anything. They had been prodigious travelers, and Calisto had known them to be brave. They died on one of their trips when they hiked into a natural disaster. It was one of Calisto's earliest memories—right before they started spending all their time at the costume shop. Not long after, in their grandparent-specific loneliness, they'd folded Mena into their family.

Calisto put a hand to Nori's back, but she didn't seem to absorb the comfort. Instead, she sprang to her feet. "If the Time Wardens are at work, we need to let people know. I'll call a meeting of the elders." Pocket's Loose Association and Book Club of Elders wasn't a ruling body—Pocket had carefully avoided those—but they advised in difficult situations. At least, theoretically. Calisto had never seen the group call an emergency meeting.

Apparently, it was time.

The Loose Association and Book Club of Elders convened in a sitting room across town, in the home of Dr. Gillian Jacobs. She was the head of the wordhouse, and her latest pick for their regular book club meetings—Italo Calvino's *Cosmicomics*—languished on the end table, translated into several languages including Seam. Instead of digging into the nooks and crannies of an excellent read, she was serving her most bracing tea to the other members. The oldest were Adama's great-grandparents, Ndeye and Massamba. The youngest was Nori, who had brought in Calisto and their tale of Time Wardens.

In a place where time was understood to be relative by nature, becoming an elder was both a state of mind and a station in the community. Dr. Gillian Jacobs herself was early middle-aged, the first white hairs finding their way into her crown of red braids. She was destined to have a few more by the time this was over.

As she poured tea, the association went over everything they'd just learned. It hadn't been easy to hear, let alone digest. The mildly sweet tea cookies helped.

"You're sure there was nothing they wanted in the shop?" Ndeye asked.

"It was turned over, not looted," Calisto said carefully. "And . . ."

"What?" asked Ells, one of the master cobblers and resident hedge witch.

"You can tell us the truth, Calisto," Massamba encouraged.

"You can tell me *anything*," Nori reminded her child.

"I know there were no costumes for Time Wardens in the shop," Calisto said staunchly. "Mena calls people in uniforms fascisti."

"A true bundle," Dr. Gillian agreed, seeking comfort where she always did—in words and their roots.

Everyone swiveled to look at her. "That's what *fascist* means," she murmured as she put down her teacup with a clink. "A bundle of sticks, specifically a sort of rod used in Roman days to punish people who stepped out of line. Violent groups in Italy later adopted the term. Mena must have learned it from the history—well, in her case, the future—of her home."

"If there were no costumes for them, and they took nothing . . ." Ndeye started.

"What did they want?" Massamba asked, breaking a single thought between them. They had been together for such a long time. Dr. Gillian tried not to be jealous and utterly failed.

57

Calisto looked torn into several pieces by the question. Dr. Gillian offered them another digestive. "I've been keeping the time savant in the costume shop since the moonful festival," Calisto mumbled, then popped the cookie in their mouth.

Quiet shock rippled over the room, evidence that the elders were wise enough not to start shouting all at once. But they couldn't hold back entirely.

"You've been doing *what?*" Nori asked.

"He's gone now," Calisto added, as if that made things better. Dr. Gillian Jacobs would have killed—well, not *killed*, but done a spot of crime—to meet Fawkes.

"Is this true?" Ells asked, worrying the crystal in her palm. "You harbored the time savant?"

"Fawkes," Calisto and Dr. Gillian said in a soft chorus.

Calisto pierced Dr. Gillian with a questioning look. She schooled her expression. If Dr. Gillian told Calisto some of the things she knew were coming, would it help? She could confirm, from experience, that knowing too much about your future wasn't always a gift.

"That savant was always going to bring trouble on his heels," Ells said. "Those crosswinds were too strong."

"He's so young," Ndeye said, shaking her head at Ells. "Just a child."

"Everyone's a child to you," pointed out Salamasina, a retired traveler with a grey shock of hair. "At some point, we become responsible for the trouble we bring in our wake."

"Not if that trouble follows us for being who we are," Massamba said.

Dr. Gillian cleared her throat. Not that she believed in the tyranny of urgent matters, but they could pick up the philosophical threads of this conversation later. "If the Time Wardens are active, we have to assume they might try to recruit new members."

"How do they do that?" Calisto asked.

For all their clamoring to talk, none of the elders wanted to take that one. Dr. Gillian answered by default. "They steal boots from travelers in the mists and in the timelands. Nobody knows who the first Time Warden was, but they became a force by recruiting from violent groups. We believe they look for individuals who have been exposed to the presence of a traveler, who are perhaps close to figuring out our existence and are unsettled by the notion. Then they insinuate themselves."

"They encourage people to hate travelers?"

"It might not be hard work, unfortunately. There have always been people who fear the power of those who are different to upset the groundwork of their reality. And many don't want us to have a power they feel they weren't given, and fight to take it away from anyone who they believe is unfairly gifted. We think they started by going after all travelers, but more and more they target anyone whose movements or abilities appear . . . unusual."

"And you just *let them?*" Calisto asked.

"No," Salamasina said. "But that doesn't mean they're easy to fight."

"The mists of time can't be searched," Dr. Gillian said. "There was a period where Pocket was full of unease and stories of attacks, but nobody has seen a warden in a very long time."

Calisto stopped pacing around the room and fell horribly still. "What happens to the travelers? The ones whose boots they take?"

The silence was as fragile as a teacup. "In some cases, we know they kill travelers for their boots. In other cases, we never hear from the travelers again. They may have been killed, or they may have been stranded in the timelands. In most cases, we'll never know."

"What we do know," Ells said, "is that anyone wearing a pair of boots is in danger."

Calisto said one scratchy word: "Mena."

"I know," said Nori. "We'll make sure she's safe."

"We should make sure *every* traveler with a known destination is checked on and brought back to Pocket as quickly and safely as possible," Ells said.

"We'll advise a check-in at a general meeting at the inn," Dr. Gillian Jacobs said. "Assuming we're all agreed?"

Everyone raised their teacups—except Ndeye and Massamba.

"You don't want to check on travelers?"

"Of course I do," she said.

"Of course we do," he echoed. "But you are speaking as if Pocket itself is safe. The Time Wardens just marched down from the hills this morning and raided one of our shops."

"They were looking for the time savant, and he's gone," Ells said gruffly. "The rest of us will be safe right here, like we've always been."

"You want to keep us safe by leaving Fawkes out there, alone?" Calisto asked. "He's being *hunted* by Time Wardens!"

"Someone's getting overwrought," Salamasina pointed out with a prim finger in the air. "*This* is why we keep youths out of the association."

"Second vote," Dr. Gillian said. "Who advises sending our own people out after travelers? *Including* a warning for the time savant?"

Everyone in the association raised their pinkies—which meant they

60

were still considering the matter. "We'll need to talk this through more thoroughly," Dr. Gillian said with a sigh.

Calisto crashed their cup on their saucer. "I thought you would help Fawkes."

"These things take consideration," Dr. Gillian said. "Consideration takes time."

Calisto spun to leave.

"Where are you going?" Nori asked.

"I'll be in the shop," they called back over their shoulder. "I can't just stand here and drink tea and do nothing."

The conversation picked up as soon as Calisto made their exit, but Gillian couldn't focus on the volley of voices as the elders argued. She was busy wishing she had a way to contact her favorite oracle and tell them that—as usual—time had proven them right.

Fawkes and Calisto were in each other's orbits.

SEVEN

Calisto sat in the ruins of the shop, sorting costumes into three piles: trampled, shredded, and destroyed. The grief of seeing Mena's work taken apart was keen enough, but each wounded garment was a sharp reminder of what might have happened if wardens had found Calisto under the cutting table with a pair of time boots.

What would happen to Fawkes if they caught *him*? Calisto tried to focus on what could be mended, but now that they'd asked this question, others followed. If the Time Wardens had been trailing Fawkes secretly throughout his youth, why would they dare to be seen now? It was one thing to lurk in the mists, but to march straight into Pocket? Was it just because they thought he was here in the costume shop alone, undefended?

A knock sounded at the front door.

Calisto whipped the shears out of their belt loop and cracked the door. The stranger on the street wasn't wearing a uniform. In fact, he was dressed down—*all* the way down—in butter-soft sweatpants, a grey T-shirt, a denim overshirt, and white puffy shoes that, on second glance, were time trainers.

"Sorry." Calisto tucked the shears into their belt. "I don't usually threaten travelers."

"I like your ferocity," the stranger replied in English. "You look ready for battle."

"I'm not ready for anything," Calisto admitted, switching to English. "And neither is the shop at the moment. We're closed."

The stranger looked over Calisto's shoulder. "Oh, they did a number on this place."

"You know about the Time Wardens' attack?"

"Of course." The stranger slipped inside. "I've been sent to ask you when Fawkes, otherwise known as the time savant, went, so I can check on him."

Relief pulsed through Calisto, throbbing their sore fingertips, still coarsely numb from sewing Fawkes's costumes. The elders must have started asking travelers to go out after Fawkes, and Mena, and anyone else wearing boots.

The stranger cast a curious glance, taking in the scope of the wreckage. "I should introduce myself. My name is Korsika. Omen Korsika."

"*Omen?*" Calisto asked, wondering if they had misheard somehow.

He laughed. "My mother thought Owen sounded nice, my father found it too bland, and here we are. Hard to say if it was a triumph of individuality or a toxic insistence on taking it too far. The line can be so thin. People from my hometime do love to walk it like a high wire. I go by Korsika."

"I'm Calisto."

"Pronouns?"

"In English? They."

"He for me." Korsika switched to Seam unsteadily. "Of course, that's only in languages that care about that sort of thing." Seam had a pronoun for strangers, another for new acquaintances, one for people you know well, a different one for those you'd known all your life. Calisto wondered, with a quick flash, which word Fawkes used for them. Which one they should use for him.

Korsika drew their attention with a smile that curved in a subtle, charming fashion. "My Seam is shaky, but I do like the way it works. People in Pocket have good ideas."

"There are languages in the timelands that don't stitch genders onto everything like unnecessary buttons." Calisto couldn't remember a single instance in their life when they'd spontaneously defended the timelands. This Korsika person seemed to put them on the wrong footing. "When travelers created Seam, they didn't do it from scratch."

"Yes, but did anyone crack time travel like you did here?" Korsika stood at the center of the room, somehow forcing Calisto to the edge of their own shop. "Centuries of clever stories, no real results. H. G. Wells and his souped-up bicycle. How about the DeLorean? Time machines of all derivations and dimensions, everyone looking for a vehicle that could *traverse* time instead of realizing that our perceptions *create* time. Therefore we must *be* the vehicle! The right technology just makes the journey reliably repeatable. Of course, Pocket is the only place where you can get *these*." He tapped his time trainers together at the heels.

"I've never worn time boots," Calisto said. The boots Fawkes gave them were still in the bag, where they would remain, a token of their strange meeting and nothing more.

"Such a shame," the traveler said with a tutting sound. "Calisto. Korsika. Our names seem to be attached to epic destinies, don't they?"

Calisto gave him a scouring look. "I'm afraid you don't look dressed to meet your destiny."

"You're probably right," Korsika said. "I dress for hard work. I don't indulge myself in fashion."

Had this person truly walked into a costume shop and denounced their art? Mena would have kicked him out, quicker than a sneeze. But Calisto wanted someone to make sure Fawkes was safe. They decided to educate this traveler, instead.

"Fashion isn't a description of fancy clothes. It's a verb. We all fashion ourselves. When you put on any outfit, you're saying something to yourself and the people around you. You're making yourself visible out of the available materials. You admitted that your clothes show you're working too hard to care about anything else. That's a powerful message to send with your sweatpants."

Korsika looked impressed, eyebrows lofted. "I must say, no one your age I've met in my own time talks quite like that. You're a delight." Calisto didn't understand why this Korsika person had to give compliments by dismissing other people in the same breath. But they didn't exactly *hate* being a delight.

"Maybe there is more to this costume business. Here's a challenge. Put me in something that changes me, and I will change my mind."

"It will have to be something Elizabethan," Calisto said.

"Can you be more specific?" Korsika asked. "The Elizabethan era is a whole queen's worth of time."

"Fawkes is going to the opening of *A Midsummer Night's Dream*."

Calisto was glad they could point to a specific event. "And a brand-new Elizabethan costume would take quite a lot of work to whip up, even without the state of the shop." They didn't want to waste a moment. The Time Wardens were on the move—who knew how long it would take until they caught up to Fawkes?

Korsika crossed to the fitting room. "Don't worry. I'm happy to wear off-the-rack. Or floor." He surveyed the littered costumes, then pointedly shut the door.

Calisto was slightly exhausted by Korsika's presence. He seemed to poke holes in everything they said and then leave them running to plug things. The sooner they gave him a costume, the sooner he'd be gone, and the sooner Fawkes would be safe. He'd have to come back to Pocket—if not right away, then at some point. Otherwise, how were they going to have the epic friendship he'd apparently foreseen?

In the back room, Calisto found the costume Mena had been working on for the perpetually annoyed Elizabethan traveler. It was mostly finished, and like all of Mena's work, glorious. It was silly to let it sit unused. Mena would find that wasteful. Calisto brought the small heap of clothes to the fitting room and slid them under the curtain.

Korsika came out only a few moments later, striding through the ruined shop. Lamplight soaked into the sumptuous silks and brocades. Calisto had expected the doublet and cloak to need a pinch of tailoring, but they hung perfectly.

"You are . . . right," Korsika admitted, checking himself in every mirror. "I do feel different. Not quite reborn, but mostly because newborns would look ridiculous in this. I'm won over. Just don't tell anyone from my hometime."

He frowned down at the bit that didn't match: the puffy white time trainers.

"I'm sorry I can't give you time boots to complete the look," Calisto said.

"Not to worry. Soon I'll be able to switch them out with ease." From an inside pocket, he plucked a piece of paper covered in mathematical scribblings.

"What is that?" Calisto asked faintly.

"The formula to make time boots, of course."

"Where did you get . . ." Their voice dwindled to nothing.

"Where else? The temporal cobblers. I'd been working on my own calculations, and I was *so* close to cracking it, but I couldn't wait anymore. So I borrowed these."

The floor of the costume shop didn't feel as solid as it always had under Calisto's feet. "The temporal cobblers would never *hand out* those equations."

"Of course not. But you see, I'm very good at making friends. Like one of the master cobblers, Ells I believe her name is."

Ells would never cough up a line of those formulas—not to an apprentice, let alone a stranger. "Did you steal them from the safe?"

"Not at all," Korsika said, looking offended. "I used my own particular talents."

"And those are . . . ?" They put their hand on their shears.

"Temporal in nature," Korsika said, brandishing a wide smile. "I may have been the one to lead the wardens here, I am sorry. But you'll have so much new business to thank me for soon. I'll tell everyone to come to Pocket and ask for *Calisto*."

They pinned him with a glare.

"I'm afraid I don't have time for your somewhat justified anger."

Korsika moved to leave. "I have to catch up with Fawkes. I've been tracking him since I learned about his unique abilities, you'll find that I'm very persistent. I'm working hard to give everyone what they deserve." He paused. "Don't you want to know what everyone deserves?"

Calisto might have given up Fawkes's destination, but they would not keep playing whatever part Korsika had assigned them. They stayed silent.

"*Time travel*, of course. Did you think you could keep it to yourselves forever?" Korsika re-pocketed the slip of paper with an unnecessary flourish. He rushed out, the cloak's hem swirling over the stoop, the rich brocade glinting in the light.

EIGHT

The moment after Korsika left the shop, Calisto learned what some people take their entire lives to understand: staying still is a choice.

They could have finished cleaning up the costume shop and pretended that Fawkes and Korsika had never come through. They could have tried to forget about Fawkes, who wasn't just stumbling through his life but was also being tracked by troubling forces.

Calisto took the time boots out of the canvas bag, thumped them on the floor, and shoved their feet in. *How* had Fawkes guessed their size? They bent to lace the boots, fingers flying, dusting the old leather with quick swipes. There wasn't time to clean them properly.

Not if they were going to catch up.

Calisto grabbed their many-scrap cloak and ran out of the shop, stopping to lock the door behind them.

They followed Korsika into the hills. Calisto readied themself to dodge into a convenient bush or take refuge behind an alpaca, but Korsika never looked back.

His pace was brisk, but Calisto's fury kept them fueled. There was no question of whether or not they could keep up as he climbed. The question was whether or not they could keep track of him between Pocket and the timelands. The path from the valley to Shakespeare's day might be well-trodden, but Calisto had never paid attention to directions that led travelers safely through the mists. Their head was full of stitches and seams, tricks of measurement and secrets of elaborate construction.

They had one hope—to follow Korsika's footsteps. Fawkes had followed the travelers on their way to the moonful festival, so theoretically it *could* be done. But that wasn't the same thing as Calisto feeling confident that they would get it right.

Losing his trail would mean wandering hopelessly, just like Calisto had been afraid Mena might. The mists could turn them around so fully that they'd struggle to find a way out. If they did reach the timelands, they could pop out anywhere. In the middle of a war. At the height of a coup. During a time when people hated science or feared magic, both of which could spell doom for travelers. And of course, they could be hunted by the Time Wardens, who would very possibly kill for the boots they'd just put on their feet.

Korsika stopped at the edge of the valley. He parted his hands as if he were master of the mists—which would have been laughable if he didn't seem to believe he could bend everything to his will. He stepped in, vanishing at once.

Calisto couldn't spare a moment for fear.

They dove in and entered a pearled abyss of nothingness. Korsika had already passed out of sight. Calisto rushed after him, their movements muffled by this non-place. Every direction looked the same. They took a step. Another. Something caught their eye, a touch of color in this blank space. Every step left a soft imprint in the pale ground with an oily rainbow swirled through it.

Right next to Calisto's imprints was a larger set. Korsika's trainers.

Calisto moved steadily, following the imprints through this utter lack of a landscape. The mists seemed like shining veils now, parting as Calisto walked, closing behind them, shushing all sound, and glowing from some unseen source of light.

Within ten steps, they felt sure they'd never find their way to this play that Fawkes was attending. Within twenty steps, they felt sure they'd never find their way home. And for what—a traveler they'd met once at a festival? But meeting Fawkes had unlocked something. Without noticing it, they had started to fashion a new idea of what their life might become.

It was a feeling as great and terrifying as the mists of time themselves.

The steps in front of them changed course, and Calisto got the vague sense that they were getting closer. It was an instinct, a sort of inner measuring, born of a life spent looking at lengths of fabric and figuring out where to snip.

Here was the final footstep that Korsika had taken. There were no more to follow. Calisto's plan frayed, panic set in. They had to follow this footstep out of the mists and into the timelands—but how?

Tiye had once described leaving the mists as *making a grand entrance into the world*. It had seemed like a metaphor, but maybe . . . Calisto put up both hands and took hold of the thinnest edges of what had seemed insubstantial.

They wrenched the edges open like curtains.

Calisto burst out of the mists.

After a few steps, they stopped short. They were standing opposite the Globe Theatre, which stood even taller than the Inn of All Ways. It was whitewashed and crossed with wooden beams, its top open to the foul London air. The city's gates were visible in the distance. The mud and fish stink of the Thames snuck up on Calisto, then overpowered them. Calisto pulled their cloak tight around their face, glad for the extra warmth. This place was mild and bone-chilling at once.

If moving through the mists of time felt intense in its sheer blankness, stepping into Elizabethan England was the opposite. Smells, sounds, sensations exploded with the violence of fireworks. Calisto thought about Fawkes, who was both gentle and skittish. Was he all right in this elbowing, shouting, stinking crowd shouldering toward the Globe?

Calisto followed the pulsing flow of people through the gates, looking for Fawkes. He wasn't dressed like the groundlings in their undyed linen and rough-spun. Calisto looked upward at the galleries above, rings of seats for the rich and noble. Their clothes were markedly brighter, garishly color-matched. Women's gowns were bedecked with gold braid, fattened with farthingales, and trimmed in furs. On noblemen, Calisto caught sight of peascods and winged shoulders with pickadils, jackets whose cuffs vomited lace. Everywhere Calisto spotted the garish architecture of ruffs—triple ruffs and fan-shaped ruffs, cartwheel ruffs and ruffs trimmed with cutwork and edged with bobbin lace points.

It was too much.

Calisto wasn't just drowning in detail but dizzy from temporal displacement. Richard had described jet lag, and this felt like a more powerful cousin. Calisto stumbled with the sheer force of it, more alarmed still to be eye level with codpieces. They bobbed back to their feet. At least adding a little dirt to their outfit helped them blend in.

Even the theater itself didn't seem as grand as Calisto had expected. It was tall but grimy, and the construction looked as if it had been thrown up in a rush. Calisto remembered, with the off-hand precision of a historian's child, that Richard had mentioned dubious wooden beams that would burn during a performance following a cannon misfire. Assuming everything played out as it always had.

Any number of things could shift, nudging the known events of the timelands into a slightly new configuration. This was one tricky part of time travel that Calisto had never had to bother with. A great sickness could wash over London—plague was no stranger to this city. A single lamp ill lit or match struck drunkenly could send rows of shoddily made buildings up in flames.

Calisto had to find Fawkes, get him out, and get home.

The play began, the actors assembling onstage, a few Greek columns hinting at the Athenian setting. Verses about love and magic—and how those forces change in an instant—rose above the clamor, art drowning out all the most horrible sensations. Even in this grim place, Shakespeare's words cast their spell. Calisto got wrapped up in them and almost forgot to keep looking.

People were starting to turn as they passed. Was it Calisto's tailor outfit, which had stood out back in Pocket and here made their presence painfully obvious? Was it the fact that they could boast only an eighth as much body odor as the rest of these people?

"Fawkes?" Calisto hissed, feeling desperate, not wanting to shout because Korsika was here—somewhere. When the scenery changed, new actors poured in from the tiring-house at the back. New actors, one of them wearing strange boots.

Fawkes was *onstage*.

They had reached one of the scenes featuring the rude mechanicals, the workers who came together to put on a play within the play. Fawkes tramped haplessly across the most famous stage in history like it was just another stumble through time.

The funniest part was, he fit right in.

The players' costumes, which Calisto had expected to be rich and studied and *right*, were a grubby assortment, a complete grab bag of quality and construction. More than that, there was an explosion of anachronisms. The costume designer, if there even was one, had mostly ignored the classical Greek setting, nodding toward it with draped garments but heaping on Elizabethan flair.

Mena would have been horrified.

Fawkes was the most outlandishly dressed, but not by much. He wore a hodgepodge of the costumes Calisto had made for him: the shalwar trousers, the suit vest with the shirt beneath it somehow missing, the Elizabethan cloak, the tie worn like a jaunty scarf *again*, and the steel-toed black time boots, of course.

"Fawkes!"

He didn't break character, or maybe he didn't notice Calisto hissing at him from the yard below. They wondered briefly, dazedly, if they could claim to have costumed a play for Shakespeare. That would make this whole perilous trip to the timelands worth it when they were back in the safety of the shop. Maybe Mena would be the first to hear it when Calisto returned. Before they could grab Fawkes, escape the Globe, and pack the whole experience into a story, the scene ended.

As the actors moved toward the tiring-house, a shout came from the second-story seats. Korsika parted the crowd of nobles in one of the lofted boxes.

Fawkes looked up wildly.

"Halt there, young Fawkes!" Korsika cried, his iambic pentameter worse than his Seam. "I challenge thee to a duel on this most time-hallowed stage!" Fawkes scrambled toward the exit, but Korsika moved fast. He *leapt* over the railing, landing on the stage. "For the entertainment of all, I present an interlude of comical proportions."

The audience cheered heartily. There had been acts before the show, and more peppered throughout as interludes. They were usually violent or funny, and Korsika promised both. He gave a deep bow, unleashing his charm on the audience.

The actors looked baffled, but more like someone had rearranged the run of the show, less like someone had rearranged the order of time. They disappeared into the tiring-house, leaving Fawkes to face Korsika.

"Fawkes!" Calisto shouted up—no need to be subtle now. But Fawkes couldn't hear them over the crowd's roaring and stamping. He and Korsika were getting ready for a fight.

Korsika paced the length of the thrust while Fawkes huddled upstage. Korsika looked entirely too at home in his costume and the power it conferred. When people saw his rich robes and noble colors, they didn't try to stop him from doing as he pleased. Calisto hated knowing they'd made that possible.

He drew a sword—Calisto hadn't given him *that*—and Fawkes found his voice.

"Good gentlepeople of the Globe, I need a weapon! With haste!"

Several nobles clamored to offer their swords for the entertainment. After a quick argument, one of them tossed down a rapier, which clattered to the stage. Fawkes picked it up and tested it, tossing it a few times, settling it in his grip.

Calisto worked their way to the stage, pressing several drunk and angry groundlings out of the way. "Fawkes!"

But Fawkes was locked in Korsika's duel. They squared off center stage, flourishing their blades. Korsika was enjoying himself. Fawkes, on the other hand, looked like he might tip over from nerves.

The fight began in earnest, and Calisto saw that they'd underestimated Fawkes. He was a wonderful fencer, light-footed and unpredictable. He slid across the stage in great swooping arcs, each stroke of the rapier clean. Korsika, however, was all bluster, waving his sword to rouse the crowd to greater heights of applause. They roared with laughter as Korsika chased a harried Fawkes.

Then Fawkes's eyes began to mist over, and Korsika lunged, all good-natured showmanship gone. His blade fell with the relentless strength of an ironmonger at the forge, white-hot with speed, sending the clattering rapier out of Fawkes's grip.

Korsika threw his sword and grasped Fawkes's wrist.

His eyes misted over, too.

It looked for all the world like Korsika was stealing Fawkes's abilities.

The robust cheers died out. Silence fell over the theater. Calisto was the only person in the Globe who knew that Fawkes was out of time.

In every sense.

They hoisted themself on the stage to instant jeers. Calisto

glanced out at the theater, sick with the weight of so many stares—
sicker to see uniforms strewn throughout the crowd. Anachronistic,
easily spotted. Flies in the ointment of time. The Time Wardens
all had the same bearing, the menacing stillness of those who only
moved when told to march, who only acted to execute orders. Their
faces were as Nori described: unidentifiable. The effect was so diz-
zying that Calisto looked down to gather themself. When they saw
their time boots, an idea sparked.

Calisto unsheathed the tailor's shears from their belt. They
walked straight to Korsika, knowing that in his misty state he
wouldn't notice. He had a tight smile, cheeks dimpled, as if whatever he was seeing courtesy of Fawkes was very good news.

Calisto stabbed him through the soft top of his time trainer.

He howled, and the white in his eyes broke fast. Fawkes returned
to the present and shook himself free of Korsika. He ran upstage
and fell into Calisto's arms. The audience crowed their approval at
what looked very much like another act of love and magic.

"Calisto!" Fawkes shouted, loud enough to light up the entire
Globe. They felt Fawkes's body in a line down their own, humming
and warm from the fight. Fawkes's dark brown eyes were grounded.
He looked wildly delighted to see them.

"You knew I was going to come?" Calisto asked, untangling the
truth.

"Yes." Before Calisto could become fully nettled, he added, "But
if I'd told you that, you might *not* have come. I didn't want a paradox
between us when we have . . . other challenges." He looked at the
doubled-over Korsika.

Then at the Time Wardens in the crowd.

"Fair enough," Calisto said.

They grabbed Fawkes's hand and led him through the tiring-house. Inside, half-dressed actors shouted as they barged through. Korsika raged and limped after them.

"Set the next scene!" someone cried. Everyone swirled to get the show going again as Fawkes and Calisto ran out the back entrance of the Globe.

They emerged onto a dusty street with the Time Wardens already coming out of the theater doors. People stared at their uniforms and their not-quite-memorable faces.

"Exit, pursued by a bundle," Calisto muttered. "Fawkes, how do we leave?"

"We need a natural boundary," Fawkes said. "Nothing human. Fog, trees, water."

"You can't fly us out?" Calisto asked, only slightly joking.

"Pocket has its own rules," Fawkes said. "And unique winds."

A strong sun had chased away any fog. There were no trees in sight. But the river lay in front of them in all of its grimy glory.

Fawkes winced.

Calisto knew what he was thinking. "Oh. No. We're not going in the Thames."

Korsika erupted from the Globe, limping on his stabbed foot, shouting—and they both made a quick but slimy journey over the muck. They splashed into the river's reedy shallows. Fawkes reached for Calisto's hand, and they used the other to seal their mouth and nose against the water's fetid, brackish stench.

They both ducked under—and plunged into the abyss.

PART TWO

NINE

Anyone who has been lost in time has felt the deepest sort of dislocation. One is tossed from any notion of here and now. It lasts moments or sighs forever. Sometimes it does both, at once. It can unmoor a person from what is known and dissolve firm beliefs. After landing with boots in thick mist, Calisto and Fawkes entered an even more potently confusing state: they became lost in time *together*.

Calisto looked down to find they were still holding hands.

They drew theirs back, then wished they hadn't. What if Calisto and Fawkes were separated from each other by the shifting curtains? Or the wardens gave chase and drove them apart? Calisto comforted themself with the strange fact that Fawkes knew they were going to be together later. Though, anything known could change. Calisto had *known*, for instance, that they would never become a traveler. And yet here they were, watching their boots create swirling imprints on the surface of time.

Fawkes walked decisively in a nothing-and-nowhere direction. If he couldn't tell where he was going to come out, how did he ever choose where to step next? Calisto stayed in one spot, stuck—then rushed to catch up, afraid to be left behind. They looked around for another set of footprints in the mist, or perhaps a trail of blood from Korsika's foot.

"I think we lost him," Calisto said.

Fawkes sighed. "I'm afraid he already got what he wanted."

Calisto frowned at the time boots Fawkes had gifted them. "So I put these on and hiked out of Pocket *for nothing*?"

"I wouldn't say that." A blush raced across Fawkes's cheeks so fast that Calisto thought they might have imagined it—or perhaps they'd been tricked by the vague, directionless light. "You did save me."

"After putting you directly in danger," Calisto muttered before they could stop themself. "Korsika came into the costume shop looking for you. I might have *accidentally* told him when you were headed."

Calisto expected Fawkes to look frustrated or betrayed. Instead, he gave a brisk nod. "You feel somewhat responsible for his destination. So do I."

"What do you mean?" Calisto asked.

"He was looking for somewhen," Fawkes said. "A spot in time. He whispered to me onstage, said he needed *a bit of assistance* to set his course. When he touched me, he found it." Fawkes rubbed the spot where Korsika had gripped his wrist. Calisto thought of Korsika's eyes misting over, his victoriously smeared smile, and they wanted to stab his foot all over again.

Fawkes sighed. "You gave him his last steps, but I gave him the next ones."

"How can you be so sure?" Calisto asked. "Did you see when he's going?"

"No, but if he hadn't seen it, he would be giving chase. He wouldn't just roar at us and give up."

"Who is this fairy tale villain?" Calisto asked. "How do you know Korsika?"

"I don't!" Fawkes cried. "But some people become obsessed with me when they find out what I can do. You know. The whole time-savant nonsense." His hands churned the air wildly. "I *have* seen that person a few times, nonlinearly speaking. I don't know how. All I know is he doesn't bode well."

"I don't need special time powers to gather that much."

"So." Fawkes turned left. "Everyone stands at a unique angle to existence." Calisto couldn't tell if this was a digression, but they would follow Fawkes—literally and conversationally—if only to avoid the sensation of going from lost to *irrevocably* lost.

"Right," Calisto said. "People have their own patch of perception."

"Local reality," Fawkes said. "That's what twenty-first-century scientists call it."

"But what does this have to do with—"

"Some local realities include a special way of understanding time. When those people travel, that relationship becomes . . . unique."

"You're saying that some travelers have special time powers?"

"I wouldn't call it that, but—"

"Like your mind-travel, but also how you move from one spot in the timelands to the next without going through Pocket . . . because your mind is moving through time already?"

Fawkes touched his temple self-consciously, as if Calisto had just peeked inside his head. "Well, yes. And I think that this Korsika can siphon other people's abilities."

"So his time power is *stealing other people's time powers*? I should have left him in sweatpants."

Fawkes took a sudden, sharp right.

"Wait," Calisto said, quickly redirecting their own steps. "Temporal cobblers have a special way of understanding time. Not everyone can become a cobbler; people can learn skills, but most of it is innate. I think that's how Korsika stole from Ells."

"He probably made contact with her—"

"—and took the secrets of time boots out of her head," Calisto finished.

"Why?" Fawkes asked. "He has a pair. Does he want to give them to someone he knows?"

"Oh, he wants *time travel for all*. Apparently, it's his grand vision."

Fawkes's free hand swirled through his dark hair, twisting a curl until it pulled free from the others. "He could have been using my mind-travel to find the right moment to introduce time boots to humanity at large."

"Oh." Calisto didn't like the sound of that. But it was none of their business. They had done what they came to do. They'd gotten Fawkes away from the people who were chasing him. "I need to go home."

They wanted nothing more than to tramp down the hill into the valley speckled with bright houses, to patch up costumes with grumbling Mena, to fall moribundly asleep, and to wake to the sounds and smells of their enormous family making breakfast.

"Back to Pocket?" Fawkes cast an eye around the abundant, misty wilds of time, clearly at a loss. "You'll have to lead the way."

Calisto didn't budge.

Travelers leaving Pocket meticulously planned their trip to the timelands. The trip *back* was supposed to be easy—reverse the directions and feel that natural, inevitable tug that had brought them to Pocket in the first place.

But Calisto hadn't followed a set of directions. They'd followed Korsika.

With a bolt of raw uncertainty turning over in their chest, they chose a direction. "I'm sure I'll start feeling the pull of Pocket when I'm nearer."

"I'll be right here." Fawkes's fingers wove between Calisto's— and tightened.

They walked on. Calisto changed directions a few times, casting around for any kind of marker, never becoming fully certain that they knew the way home.

Then they stopped.

Calisto cast quick, sharp looks around them. They still seemed to be alone with Fawkes, lost on a blank canvas of mist. And yet it felt like someone—*many someones*—were there past the small circle of their senses. Waiting, watching, hungry for a misstep.

"Change of plans." Fawkes tugged Calisto in a new direction. "We're going to the oldest era we can reach with a swift hike."

"You can't drag me—"

"Away from Time Wardens?" Fawkes asked.

"*Calisto.*"

Their name came from the blankness. It sounded like shredded mist, raspy and wrong. It was spoken by one voice, then echoed by a dozen others.

"*Calisto. Calisto. Calisto.*"

The Time Wardens knew their name. And that was enough to make Calisto run.

They ran.

And ran.

And ran.

Calisto's ankles, knees, and lungs threatened to give out at the same moment. "How *long* is human history?"

"We probably lost the wardens," Fawkes gasped. "They hate the ages where time is wild, not something they can regulate. Humanity's stranglehold on time grows tighter with overpopulation. Time zones, standardized clocks, synchronized computing. *Productivity.*" He shuddered.

"Time gets more intensely controlled as you move toward later eras?"

Fawkes shifted. "Up to a point."

Calisto dropped a pin in that for later. "Speaking of the wilds of time, how do you know we're moving toward the *past*?"

"Past and future aren't specific destinations. They're ideas. *Very* subjective."

"Is that why you never show up in Pocket? It's not past *or* future?" Nobody knew how it had happened or why the valley had detached from the rest of the timelands, but it was clearly off on its own.

Fawkes didn't answer. He was staring behind them. "One of the Time Wardens followed us. Keep moving. Don't look back."

Calisto, of course, glanced back and caught a figure trailing. He moved at a clipped gait and wore an olive drab uniform with details of polished brass. "Keep going until we reach the first cave people. We can take our chances with them."

88

Fawkes's steps slackened and slowed to a stop.

"Hey." Calisto tugged his sleeve. "Did you hear what I said?"

Fawkes had left the present, blinking with a hard flutter. His entire body went blank. Calisto looked back—and found the drab warden *much* closer. Fawkes's misty eyes cleared, and he shook his head with a spasm. When he spoke, his voice was calm. "There's a strong chance you're about to sink into the ground like quicksand."

Calisto's feet sank into the ground like quicksand.

"You couldn't have foreseen that a bit sooner? The warden is nearly on top of us."

Fawkes looked down. "At the rate we're sinking, I think we'll go under before he reaches us."

"What a comforting thought," Calisto said. "Also, what *is* this?" They tested the unsettled ground beneath their boots. It felt stickier than sand, with a thickness like the raw honey Tiye collected from her apiary. Calisto loved twirling a spoonful into their tea but not being up to their ankles in the stuff.

"It feels like some kind of trap," Fawkes said.

"A time trap?" Calisto's fear rose as they sank to their hips. The drab warden was close enough for them to see the shallow blue waters of his eyes. He stopped short of the time trap. And started to load a musket.

Calisto pushed at the trap and felt it swirl, closing tighter.

Fawkes looked more interested in testing the trap's response than escaping it. He watched it with a sort of curious remove. As Calisto fought harder and the warden worked on the long process of loading a musket, Fawkes shook his head. "Guns don't work here."

"*He* doesn't seem to know that."

Calisto was in up to their chest, being dragged ever downward. The warden aimed the musket at their head. *Fired.* Calisto flinched, then opened their eyes to see the ball cut the mist and vanish.

"Bullets emerge in random spots in the timelands," Fawkes said matter-of-factly.

"That's worrisome information, and you already don't seem worried enough," Calisto told Fawkes as the time trap reached their neck. The drab warden took a frustrated step, getting snared in the trap, too.

"Worry won't change our trajectory," Fawkes said. "Why bother?"

"I think I hate time travel." Calisto sank to their pointed-up chin. "Or time travel hates me."

"I'm sure it's nothing personal," Fawkes grinned, right as Calisto went under.

They emerged in a grove of trees. The earth reconfigured itself, from honeyed time-mist to hard-packed earth. Sunlight broke through dark green leaves, helping Calisto shake off the sticky feeling of the time trap and the cold fear of the drab warden.

Fawkes and Calisto stumbled to the edge of the grove. They were near a city, one with buildings hewn from great blocks of beige sandstone. The air hung thick with herbal perfume from trees, all of which looked like the ones in the grove, gnarled and windscaped. Calisto felt at home in a way they hadn't in the overstuffed Elizabethan era. At least this metropolis had wide avenues, gardens, and open stretches of countryside.

"Knossos," Fawkes whispered. "Crete. Probably around 1500 BCE."

"Why would someone set a trap for travelers to come *here?*" Calisto asked.

"Your guess is as educated as mine," Fawkes said. "The question I keep circling around is *who* set it."

Calisto felt a prickle of hope. There had to be another traveler on Crete. Someone who'd come from Pocket. Someone who could help Calisto get home. They didn't want to move forward without a plan, but the warden would come through the trap at any moment. "Let's find somewhere to hide until it's safe to get out of here."

Fawkes and Calisto headed toward the city. "Do you speak Minoan?" Calisto asked, remembering how easily Fawkes had strung together various languages.

"No Minoan. But maybe a root language? And Crete is trading pretty widely by this time, I think. I should know a language or two that someone would recognize. Maybe."

"*You think? Maybe?* Have you never been here before?" Calisto had started to think that Fawkes had been just about everywhen.

He didn't get a chance to answer. A small group approached swiftly. Calisto pinned them as soldiers or guards. "More uniforms," they muttered.

Their outfits did support Fawkes's stab at a date. If they'd landed any later than 1500 BCE, military types would have sported bronze as plate armor or mail in the Persian style. These were earlier options, cuirasses and shields reinforced with leather. Below the outfits' skirted bottoms, the soldiers' bare legs showed off highly athletic sandals.

Fawkes strode toward the group—still sporting what he'd worn onstage at the Globe. He had looked eccentric in *A Midsummer Night's Dream*, but under the strong ancient sun, he was like a hallucination.

Calisto couldn't imagine how their outfit looked. They were wearing a great deal of wool, which people in this time had in abundance. That was where the similarities came to a screeching halt.

After a quick back-and-forth among the Cretans, one soldier stepped forward to speak directly with Fawkes. Before Calisto could get too excited, a distinct thump and rustle came from the grove behind them.

The drab warden tumbled out.

The soldiers spooked and raised their spears. They circled Fawkes, Calisto, and the warden. They bound wrists and pointed the prisoners toward the city, prodding them to walk. With a shout, one of the soldiers grabbed the warden's musket and inspected it. At least he didn't have a gun anymore. And he couldn't chase Fawkes and Calisto if they were all prisoners.

Pretty dull, as far as silver linings went.

Fawkes spoke in hushed, tight tones. "They've been instructed to keep an eye out for anyone wandering out of that grove, wearing . . . strange outfits."

"Interesting." That would make sense if other travelers had come through, which gave Calisto hope. It was instantly tempered by the idea that those travelers might have been captured by soldiers, too.

The drab warden marched behind Fawkes and Calisto. They twisted to look and found his face just as unsettlingly forgettable up close. What did he look like to the Cretans? A fellow soldier?

They passed cobbled streets that led to a palace. It bore great pillars painted bright red and murals in earth tones depicting religious activities. They passed a massive ring of an amphitheater, and terraced gardens that led into deep pits of earth and greenery. It would have been impressive without the wafting sense of doom.

"Fawkes, please tell me what they are doing."

The guard behind Calisto poked them in the back.

"They're bringing us to the labyrinth," Fawkes whispered. "To fight the monster that lives at its heart."

TEN

Fawkes and Calisto faced the fabled labyrinth of Crete. Great doors rose before them, pitted slabs of black stone. A cloud of flies buzzed. Two guards moved forward to haul the doors open by knobs made from animal horns. There were pools on the ground, dark and sticky, that appeared to be old blood.

Calisto looked for any way to escape this abrupt fate.

Instead, they found the drab warden staring them down, chilly and inexorable.

Fawkes and Calisto were ushered into the dark, cool mouth of the labyrinth as it exhaled a dank breath. Guards sliced the ties at their wrists. The warden was dragged in after them.

Fawkes shouted a few words in a language Calisto couldn't begin to unknot. The guards withdrew, and the doors closed with a great grinding of stone. Calisto sprang into motion, Fawkes a half step behind. The warden writhed, trying to fight off the ropes that still bound him.

"Why are we free and he's still tied up?" Calisto asked, twisting to look at the warden and then deciding it was best to focus on getting away from him. Fast.

"I asked the guards to leave him bound," Fawkes said.

"And they listened to you?" Calisto asked.

"I bet the musket convinced them he's more dangerous than we are. They think they're giving us a fighting chance."

"To beat the monster or survive the other prisoner?"

"Both?"

Fawkes and Calisto pelted down narrow stone passageways, the entire city of Knossos fading with each step.

"Is this what people do for entertainment here?" Calisto shouted, as if someone might hear their words tossed over the high walls. "They shut in people to die? I miss the Elizabethans."

"Plenty of violence passing for fun in that era," Fawkes panted as he ran. "Please don't make me describe bearbaiting."

"Speaking of violence," Calisto said, "how are we supposed to fight a monster?"

Fawkes gave Calisto an encouraging grin. "You can stab it with your shears."

"You seem to think I'm capable of anything," Calisto said. "Which shouldn't make me feel stronger, but somehow it does."

The angled walls narrowed the sky above them to a thin blue ribbon. The footsteps of the warden played tricks on Calisto—coming from behind, then the other side of the wall. "*These* are the consequences of going somewhen without the right costumes. If we'd arrived in the proper clothes, the warden would be in here and we wouldn't."

"Would you rather have the right drapey toga thing and not have any of your pins or tailor's gear?" Fawkes asked.

"First, it's called a mantle. Togas are Roman. Second, I can hide pins anywhere." Calisto took a sharp turn. Fawkes followed seamlessly. "Third, we have to make the traveler who set the time trap take us back to Pocket."

Fawkes looked up at the meager sky. "I'm not sure I'm going back."

Calisto felt a quick needle of abandonment. "Where else do you want to go?"

Fawkes shrugged. The drab warden's steps grew closer yet again. "Let's find a way out, and then we can make travel plans."

Fawkes whirled around as a new set of stone passageways stretched and branched. "Should we try the left-hand trick?"

"Turn left until we get out?" Calisto asked. They'd done it in a garden maze once with Myri and Onyx, and it had worked.

"I'll drop a thread behind us so we know which passages we've tried," Calisto said, then drooped. "But the drab warden will follow it to us like an arrow."

"Wait," Fawkes said. "Thread could work."

Calisto fished up a spool of red thread and handed it to Fawkes. He ran away, trailing it after him, and by the sound of it, he made several turns. He came back smiling, without the spool.

"That was my best crimson!" Calisto whisper-shouted.

"Yes, and the drab warden, whose name you gifted so perfectly, will follow it to a room filled with skittering scorpions. I tossed the thread over the top of a high wall. We can get far away while he's trying to follow it."

Fawkes leapt in a new direction, waving for Calisto to follow.

They ran hard, taking each left-hand turn—left, left, left again, twisting deeper into the labyrinth. The path opened from a strangled corridor into a square room with a trough of oil running down the center. The moment Fawkes and Calisto walked over the threshold, a pulley system dropped a torch that set the oil aflame. Within moments, the flames roared as high as Calisto's waist. There was no going over it. No way around.

"How do we avoid this?" Calisto asked.

Fawkes inspected the trough from all angles, close enough to roast a marshmallow. When he came back, his cheeks were ruddy, his lips flushed bright pink. Calisto pulled back, as if the flame were, in fact, Fawkes himself. "We don't avoid it," he said proudly.

"We set ourselves on fire?"

"People assume tests are about cleverness, but what if most are about patience?"

"That's a great philosophical question, but we have someone following us."

"Can you hear him right now?"

Calisto closed their eyes. "No."

"Good. I'm hungry." Fawkes crossed his legs and sat down. Calisto sat next to him. Wordlessly, Fawkes handed Calisto a small pie from the inner folds of his cloak.

"Where did you get *this*?" Calisto asked.

"From the Elizabethans. I had to trade those clothes for food."

"The clothes I made? You gave away everything I created and tailored in exchange for steaming meat packets?" Calisto asked, barely able to get the words past their indignation.

"I needed to eat." Fawkes's brow nettled as if this were painfully obvious, but the pain was doubling because he didn't want to upset

Calisto. He brightened. "If it helps, they were worth a lot of meat packets."

Calisto might have stayed angry if they had eaten since they left Pocket. The pie Fawkes held out was sealed in layers of wax and paper. Calisto took an overwhelming bite of pastry, sinking past the golden crisp and into the herbed meat. They spoke around a perfect mouthful. "It's possible that, under the circumstances, trading garments for this pie was worth it."

Fawkes pulled out another pie and touched it to Calisto's in a sort of *cheers*.

Calisto wolfed down several bites. "It's funny that you believe patience is a virtue. You're the only person I know who doesn't have to sit around and wait for their life to unfold in the usual order."

"That requires *extra* patience. I get these flickers of what's coming without knowing how or why. I have to wait for things to make sense. Then I have to wait for other people to catch up, and when they do, I'm somewhen else."

"Is that why you keep to yourself?" Calisto asked.

Fawkes nodded and tucked into his meat pie. It was probably the wrong time for questions, but the drab warden's footsteps were missing and the oil was burning slowly. Calisto needed something to think about besides whatever mythical monster was also trapped in this labyrinth.

"Where did you get these?" Calisto knocked the toes of their time boots together.

"The same place I got mine."

"Why did you give them to me?"

Fawkes slowed his bite. Calisto waited for him to say something frustrating and tautological, about how he had to offer them time boots because he knew they were going to wear those exact time boots later. Instead, he hugged his knees. "I've been lonely for a long time."

Warmth filled Calisto, and it wasn't just because the room was on fire.

"You seem lonely, too," he added.

"I have plenty of people in Pocket," Calisto noted.

"Does that erase my point?"

Calisto didn't know how to answer. Or if they wanted to.

"So you were little when you got your time boots. Where did they come from?" They kept the question vague, hoping that he might illuminate his childhood and hometime.

"The grown-up gave them to me."

"What was this person like?"

"Dark hair, wispy, time boots." Fawkes grinned. "They looked like me a little."

Calisto stopped just shy of asking if this person was Fawkes's parent. It sounded like he wasn't sure but suspected it—maybe hoped it was true. "The grown-up was a traveler?"

"Yes. They gave me boots just like their own. Kept me company. And then, they were gone, and it was only me again. Maybe I should have waited until the boots fit better to take my first trip into the mists, but I remember feeling like I couldn't stay. I stuffed the soles with leaves."

"You didn't travel to eras with socks?" Calisto asked.

Fawkes arched a single dark brow. "Eventually."

Fawkes came from a hometime more different than Calisto could stretch their mind around. No matter how far back or remote, people in the timelands tended to have more than one other person around

Which led Calisto to another question. "Why did the grown-up give you two pairs of time boots?"

Fawkes twirled one of his dark curls. It was a thinking-related habit that he tumbled into. It seemed to help him focus. "I don't know that. Not yet." He crumpled the wrapping from his pie and threw it in the fire. It flared, then died. Fawkes got up and leapt over the ankle-high flames, looking adorably satisfied with himself.

"See? Patience."

Calisto leapt, too, and they both worked their way down more grimy corridors. A scraping sound, something hard dragging against stone, moved toward them from a direction that Calisto couldn't quite pin down.

Behind them, the drab warden roared, his footsteps growing close again.

"If the drab warden's behind us, who's making that sound ahead of us?" Calisto asked.

There was only one direction they could move without turning around and facing the warden. "We're about to discover the answer," Fawkes said. "Did that scraping sound like hooves to you?"

Calisto walked hesitantly into a room with torches in brackets all around. A heap of bones lay in a pit. Hollow wing bones, the filigree ribs of small mammals, large leg joints, and others that looked human.

The drab warden made it to the threshold of the room. He slowed to a more purposeful pace now that he had Fawkes and Calisto in his sights. Stripped of his musket, the only weapon he seemed to have was bottomless wells for eyes.

Calisto fished out a seam ripper. "Stay behind me, Fawkes." As scared as they were, they could not let Fawkes be the one to deal with this warden, Fawkes who had been facing these people since he was small and alone.

"Can I help you?" Calisto asked.

"*Travelers are unnatural, a plague upon time,*" he chanted.

"You have a pair of boots on, you know," Calisto said. "You live in the mists. You're time traveling *right now.*"

"The stings of hypocrisy are lost on him," Fawkes whispered.

"*Travelers are unnatural, a plague upon time,*" the warden repeated. "*We fight until the timelands are wiped clean. You will not stop us. No one will stop us.*"

"Do they always give this monologue?" Calisto asked. "It's not Shakespeare."

"Mostly they say I endanger the one true timeline. This wiping-clean business is new."

The seam ripper shook in Calisto's grip. The drab warden advanced several steps, forcing them backward.

Behind them, the gravelly grinding of hooves filled the chamber, echoing in the pit.

"We're stuck between a monster and a monster . . ."

Calisto and Fawkes turned to face a beast swaying with slow menace. It stood behind the bone pit on two darkly furred legs, twice as tall as Fawkes. Its bull nostrils streamed smoke, its ember-colored eyes glowing in the dark room.

"*Minotaur,*" Fawkes said like he'd finally remembered. "That's what's at the center of the labyrinth!"

Fawkes and Calisto edged farther into the minotaur's chamber. The warden pursued, pushing forward, only the seam ripper stopping him from a full charge. The growing proximity to the minotaur didn't seem to give the warden pause—he only wanted to hunt travelers.

Calisto and Fawkes edged around the bone pit. They neared the minotaur, and Calisto found that its thick pelt didn't smell terrible. Underneath the smoke there was a faint floral scent, as if someone washed this monster regularly.

That distraction couldn't hold their attention for long.

The warden charged Calisto.

They held the seam ripper at arm's length, ready to stab him in the gut with what amounted to the world's tiniest pitchfork.

A low roar made them all cower. By the time Calisto looked up, the minotaur had sideswiped the warden. It propelled him into a dark passageway, where a trapdoor opened beneath the drab warden's feet. With a flash of brass rivets, he fell. The trapdoor resealed, leaving him to rot in some forgotten, lightless hole.

Calisto turned to the minotaur, brandishing the seam ripper. They weren't going to die here. They were getting back to Mena and Pocket. Back to their family, their friends, their *fabrics*. "Stay back! Stay back or I'll . . . disassemble you!"

"Please don't." The muffled voice came from somewhere around the minotaur's chest. "It took me forever and a half to make this."

Fawkes and Calisto traded tentative looks.

The minotaur huffed, and puffed, and took itself apart. Its head came off, a sort of enormous ball wrapped in animal skins. The hide came next in ragged pieces. Limbs were tossed aside by a person huddled on stilts with pulleys. A tin incense burner sat on their head, still trickling the minotaur's nose smoke.

102

If Calisto hadn't been so busy with the warden, they would have recognized this costume sooner. The construction was enviable but the hide stitches were done with an awl. Calisto could have popped them with well-placed jabs.

The person hacked a cough. "You have no idea how uncomfortable it is to be a creature of legend."

Fawkes shrugged as if maybe he did, in fact, know.

It took Calisto a moment to understand why the words had sounded both deeply strange and welcome at once. They'd been spoken in Seam.

"You're the traveler who set the time trap," Calisto said.

"You're not a minotaur," Fawkes added.

"You're Fawkes and Calisto!"

Calisto wasn't quite used to hearing their names like that. Together. As if they meant something specific and necessary. *Fawkes and Calisto.* It made them a bit dizzy, or maybe that was just the smoke hanging thick in the air.

The ex-minotaur's tunic flung and their ash-colored hair flopped as they leapt over the discarded shaggy costume. This person was older than Fawkes and Calisto but moved with the twitchy energy of youth. They ran to make sure the trapdoor had fully sealed. "Never a good sign to see a Time Warden come this far into the ancient world."

Fawkes tapped Calisto's shoulder. "That's what I said!"

"Why did he follow us?" Calisto asked.

"This is what it feels like to be special," Fawkes said wearily.

The former minotaur bundled up the costume and stashed it behind the bone pit. "We have so much to cover. So much to *do.* You'll forgive me if I move at a quick pace and forgo most of the usual introductions. I'm Kellan, a *retired* traveler and current oracle of Knossos." Kellan waved them both over, then headed down a set of stairs hidden behind the bone pit. "My personal labyrinth exit."

The stairs descended steeply, leading to an underground passage. It stretched out like an enormous earthworm's tunnel.

"These paths run all the way to Heraklion," Kellan announced over their shoulder, "but that's not where we're going."

"And where is that?" Calisto asked, a nervous edge to their voice.

"Home."

ELEVEN

In all their time on Crete, Kellan had never had houseguests. Or to put it precisely—as their favorite linguist would have appreciated—hutguests.

"Here we are." After a tramp through tunnels and up a lofty hill, they arrived at a tiny edifice with whitewashed walls, a tiled roof, and bright strands of bougainvillea. "Home sweet oracular hut."

"This is where you live?" Calisto asked.

"And work! People like oracles to be out of the way. Adds to the mystique."

"How does a traveler end up as an oracle in ancient Crete?"

"Oh, the usual." Kellan led them inside and gave the incredibly brief tour of the single room with its straw pallet and hearth. "After leaving my hometime, I worked across eras. Predicted storms on the high seas for pirates who plundered colonizers. Charmed prim Victorians with my connections to the unseen. Made a stop as an early circus performer, but I never got used to rude audiences and sad-eyed elephants. Spent some time in Pocket, naturally. But the perks of being an ancient soothsayer are real."

They'd found a place where their gifts weren't just tolerated or treated as a diversion but treasured by those who wished to pick out the patterns of the universe. And after a heartbreak or two, they'd needed the kind of quiet only the ancient world could provide.

Calisto was upending that hard-earned peacefulness, riffling through Kellan's few possessions.

"What are you doing?" they asked.

"Looking for your time boots." Calisto cast a glance at Kellan's bare feet. "We need you to take us to Pocket."

"I'm afraid that's not where you need to go next. You two are ready to take leaps in becoming who you have always been."

"No tortured time logic, please," Calisto said.

Kellan put water on the hearth for hot drinks. "Put plainly, you are here to become a pair of great travelers."

Fawkes beamed at that.

"And it's a bit urgent," Kellan added.

"A pair?" Calisto asked. "People hardly ever travel in pairs, and I only left Pocket to keep Fawkes safe from a villain in sweatpants who was hunting him as part of some inane plan to become the lord of time boots."

Kellan winced at the *Korsika* of it all. "Neither Pocket nor the timelands are safe as long as he is out there trying to act as if he invented time travel, selling Korsika-brand boots to anyone who can afford them."

"Why do you seem so upbeat, then?" Calisto asked suspiciously.

"Because I set up a pothole in the mists to keep watch for you two, and here you are. There's quite a lot to talk about, beginning with when I first met you, Calisto."

The water in Kellan's kettle boiled just as the ground began to shake. They swung it out of the fire and grabbed the doorframe. "But first, hold on."

The island shook every atom in Kellan's bones. It only lasted a few vicious moments.

They still had time.

Kellan looked over to their young charges to find that they'd stayed on their feet by grabbing ahold of each other. Fawkes and Calisto disentangled their limbs with a bashfulness that seemed to occur to them after the fact.

Kellan pointedly ignored that.

"Was that an earthquake?" Calisto asked, shaking off shivers. "I've never felt one."

"I have," Fawkes said, "and they've never felt like that."

"There's seismic activity aplenty here." Kellan looked out at a sun-ridden landscape that people had turned into grazing land and gardens but never quite tamed. "These new quakes are shaking the very stuff of reality. Time is trying to branch."

"Oh," Fawkes said quietly.

"How is that possible?" Calisto asked.

"What do you know about branching?" Kellan asked.

Calisto frowned. "Travelers come through Pocket and tell us about things that got altered in the timelands. A life saved here, a fire started there. Most branchings cause a ripple in the air. A shivering sense that something shifted. *That* was much too big."

"I agree," Kellan said. "The flow of time is a collective force, not

107

the work of storied individuals. Every human experience braided together becomes annoyingly resilient. Daily travelers who tried to create change by stopping an important figure or altering a crucial moment found themselves disappointed when another figure stepped in and a new moment popped up to fill its place."

"Like mushrooms," Fawkes supplied.

"It taught travelers to value the tangible good that came from little changes, instead of the pompous hope of becoming time-walking saviors. But . . ." Kellan went around, checking the solidity of their hut. There were a few cracks, and they got to patching, shoving mud into place. "Large branches *are* possible, in rare cases. Korsika has been chasing one. He's closing in."

"No wonder Time Wardens are after him." Fawkes pitched in with the hut repairs. "They're obsessed with the idea of the one true timeline."

Kellan sighed. "Korsika needs to be dealt with before he mucks up everywhen. If the Time Wardens catch him and have their way . . . I wouldn't buy tickets to that particular apocalypse."

Calisto sat on the floor, looking dizzier in the aftermath of the quake than during the event itself. "You're saying that we have to stop Korsika and the Time Wardens. What if I don't want anything to do with this? What if I make a different choice?"

"*Destiny* is a word that people who experience their lives in a limited order use for things they've *already chosen*. Just because you haven't chosen it yet doesn't mean it's being thrust upon you."

Fawkes's smile filled the hut. "Destiny is a temporal disorder!"

"Exactly," Kellan said. "Don't believe in destiny, believe in yourself. Ugh, that sounds like a motivational poster."

"What's a poster?" Calisto asked.

"Do you want to keep working on that motto?" Fawkes said. "I can help!"

Kellan wilted under the weight of this conversation and their responsibilities all at once. "Listen, I'm new to the mentor business. I've been on my own for a very long time, and I'm not used to inspiring people. I usually tell someone when to harvest their crops or proclaim their love or launch a small army. They give me honey, some soft cheese, a few casks of wine, and we call it a day." Kellan finished patching the wall and returned to the kettle.

Calisto accepted a mug of steaming tea. "I wanted to get back to Pocket to make sure everyone I love is all right. Which they won't be if Korsika is out there. I think some part of me already knew that."

"So you're ready for temporal lessons?"

Calisto looked down at their boots, then over at Fawkes. "Yes."

There wasn't a speck of time to waste. "Let's get started, shall we?" Kellan sat as their eyes went white with mist.

Fawkes's entire life stuttered. He had never *watched* anyone time travel within the confines of their own head. To another person, it might have triggered an inner alarm system—something strange, something wrong.

To Fawkes, it brought a flood of comfort.

He sat down in front of cross-legged Kellan and stared unabashedly into the oracle's shifting white eyes. The mists looked like clouds moving across the sky with peace and purpose.

The oracle mind-traveled with an ease that Fawkes never felt, ripped out of one moment and deposited in a new one, only to be torn out of *that* reality and tossed into the straitjacket of linear progression. When he returned, it felt hard to stay, to hold on to what was happening in this slippery moment.

When Kellan came back, they sprang to their feet in a way that defied the concept of ankles. They didn't look like they were shaking off the sticky residue of some other moment. They didn't seem half-stuck, stranded between realities. They didn't look haunted by whatever they had seen. They were *refreshed*.

"I call those my mind-walks," Kellan said.

"When did you go?" Fawkes asked.

"As a first task, I need to help you learn to anchor yourself to the present, Fawkes. You must stay connected to your body in order to wander farther afield in time. It's been a long while since I had to think about how this works. I was casting myself back to the first time I found an anchor for my mind-walks."

"What kind of anchor?"

"Whatever keeps you calm and grounded. It can change over time, but it must be powerfully important to you. Right now, my anchor is this landscape. My chosen home."

Fawkes felt his smile slide away. "I've lived in a lot of places, not exactly by choice."

"There are other types of anchors," Kellan promised.

"What do I need to learn?" Calisto asked.

"I'll show you, but for now, get some rest. You two look quite drained. Here is a blanket . . ."

Calisto grabbed it and curled up on a mat. Fawkes hovered, shifting from time boot to time boot. "Come on," they said. "You must be exhausted."

"There's not a lot of hut."

"We'll fit," Calisto said with certainty.

As Kellan left to do whatever oracles did at night—consulting with the moon or asking the stars what to call them—Fawkes curled up carefully on the mat and pulled the blanket over Calisto, settling it under their chin.

"You belong under the blanket, too," Calisto said, words soft with onrushing sleep. "C'mere."

Calisto flung out an arm and drew Fawkes close with a small noise of contentment in their throat. He settled against the crescent of their body. Stretches of his skin discovered theirs. Each tiny motion as they held each other tighter brought them into new contact. Each shift turned Fawkes breathless.

Calisto's breathing evened, deepened.

They were drifting off.

Fawkes wasn't ready to leave this moment for the darkness of sleep. He was too excited. Traveling by Calisto's side made Fawkes feel brightness and calm. Being pressed together like this brought on both feelings in such large amounts that he could barely contain them.

As the single silver moon rose over Crete, casting its searchlight through the open door of the hut, the mist came over him gently, like another blanket falling around his shoulders. He mind-walked to the moment he met Calisto at the festival.

A constant, bright as the moon.

TWELVE

Calisto woke to a bold sun and Fawkes tugging at their arm. "Come on!" he said, trying to haul them from the ground as they groaned. Calisto wasn't ready to leave behind their deep and glorious sleep.

"What are we doing?" they asked.

"A test! I've been waiting. You slept hard." Fawkes was tugging at dark curls with both hands, twirling his way through some kind of epiphany. His excitement was catching, but Calisto's head spun with the smells that filled the hut.

"Breakfast first, please."

Kellan was nowhere to be seen. Spread on the floor beside Fawkes and Calisto was a small feast in pottery covered with the calligraphy of differential equations: not just handmade but Kellan-made. There were rusks, soft cheese in pools of honey, quail eggs in cream, and a thickly brewed, coffee-like substance that tasted like bitter twigs.

Kellan came in, looking delighted to find that they'd decimated the food together. "Here," they said, holding out squares of linen along with a handful of gold trim. "I asked my contacts at the palace for material to outfit yourselves for this era."

"Thank you." Calisto felt better as soon as they accepted the stack of fabric.

"I can also get you access to a flush toilet! There's only one on the island, but they're quite ahead with the engineering."

Fawkes ran out of the hut.

"He's eager to get started," Calisto explained, heading for the door. The oracle settled in on a floor pillow and looked like they were staying put. "Aren't you giving Fawkes mind-walk lessons today?"

"I also need to eat. Besides, I get the sensation that you two could use a moment to yourselves." They clutched a clay mug of the coffee-like substance, smiling over its rim. Their grin was a little *too* knowing.

"I keep being the last one to find out about things," Calisto said, frustration rising fast. "So if you're aware of something about me and Fawkes that you're not saying . . ."

Kellan held up both hands in innocence. "As an oracle, many of my predictions are grounded in the here and now — and last night — when you and Fawkes made yourselves as cozy as two barn kittens."

The memory of Fawkes's warmth worked its way through them, leaving a head-to-toe flush in its wake.

Calisto shot Kellan a mortified look. "What kind of mentor are you?"

"The kind that remembers being young!" Kellan shouted as they left the hut.

Fawkes was moving fast, and Calisto scudded down the steep trail after him. When they reached the end, they found themself standing on a steep sea cliff. They hadn't gotten a good glimpse of the sea during the hike to Kellan's hut. It was right here. It was *everywhere*. The sea looked as mighty as the mists, a grand patchwork of shifting blues and seething power.

Fawkes seated himself at the exact edge of the cliff. He looked like a mirror of Kellan, cross-legged and loose-limbed.

Calisto claimed a spot among the roots of a nearby cypress, whipping out a measuring tape and pins. They left their shears untouched. In this era, the linen that created their tunics and mantles should remain uncut, shaped by skillful folding, draping, and pleating. Calisto dove into the challenge with uncomplicated pleasure.

Fawkes stared out at the far-off, hazy place where sea melted into sky. "Remember in the shop when you were working on costumes, you wanted to know what my next destination would be?"

"You didn't tell me you had a destination until *after* I'd made half a costume." Calisto gathered fabric, relieved to have something to do with their hands—and something to stare at other than Fawkes's profile sketched against the backdrop of the cliffs.

"When you asked me, I got a flash of being at the play. Like I had some say over when I was mind-walking."

"You think *I'm* your anchor?" Calisto asked, the idea tumbling out.

"There's a way to find out." Fawkes's fingers tapped his knees in an excited, nervous rhythm, a code that Calisto couldn't quite follow. "Ask me when Korsika is going next."

"All right. When is Korsika going next?"

Calisto squinted hard at Fawkes, waiting for his eyes to mist over.

"Why are you staring at me like that?" Fawkes asked, blinking with a rare burst of self-consciousness.

"I'm waiting for you to mind-walk!" Calisto said.

"Me too." Fawkes took a deep breath. "You asked me when Korsika's going, but you have to want to *know*."

"I do. I just also want to go—"

"Home." Fawkes's face folded. Calisto thought of how much it hurt to know that Mena wanted to leave the costume shop and return to her hometime, to a place they could never belong.

"It's time to try this on," Calisto said.

Fawkes unbuttoned the suit vest and shucked it from his shoulders. Calisto hadn't calculated *how* shirtless he was beneath that bespoke waistcoat. His skin glowed brown in Crete's unabashed sun. Freckles swirled across his shoulders.

They stared. For costuming purposes.

Fawkes must have felt the weight and texture of Calisto's attention because he looked over and cocked his head. "You're comfortable with naked because you worked in a costume shop. Right?" Uncertainty turned him pink. "I forget not all whens are comfortable with naked."

"Pocket is not just any *when*," Calisto said. "And yes, I'm used to seeing people in various states at the shop." That was only half the story, though. They didn't know how to explain that this wasn't the fitting room experience they were used to—and Fawkes's body wasn't a random traveler's personal and uninteresting business.

Fawkes was *Fawkes*.

They dropped the tunic over his head, making only the briefest contact with his skin. Even that felt intense, as if the slight graze left a searing in their fingertips. Calisto put their hand to their lips.

Fawkes continued, his head swallowed in fabric. "I'm comfortable being naked because there were no real clothes when I came from. I dressed as a wild animal all childhood. Or, I guess, undressed." His head came through the fold with a winning and wolfish grin.

"Were you a caveman?" Calisto asked. "That would explain a few things."

"No caves. I lived in great big trees."

Calisto didn't really take that as a no.

"What do you think?" he asked, smoothing the linen over the planes of his body, looking up at Calisto for approval.

There was something missing—just not in the costume.

"How are we going to catch Korsika if you can't move through time with purpose?" Their thoughts moved in looping circles as they folded their own tunic in aggressively straight lines. "That's *not* like the play because you landed in the Elizabethan era by accident."

Fawkes shrugged in the heedless way that had bothered Calisto at first. They were starting to understand that he'd never learned to care about his safety because no one had taught him it was worth caring about. Maybe that was why he didn't hesitate to dive into the mists after Korsika. Or argue with them while standing on a literal cliff's edge.

"I'd feel more confident as your anchor if I knew you could travel with some ability to navigate. Otherwise, we won't be able to reach Korsika, and the Time Wardens will be waiting for us."

Fawkes closed one eye against the bold sun, squinting the other at Calisto. "Are you holding your assistance hostage?"

"Absolutely."

He tilted his head back and growled with pure exasperation. Calisto tried not to laugh at how adorable it sounded.

This was serious.

"It's called a *condition*, Fawkes," Calisto said. "To keep us from rushing headlong into danger. I broke the only condition my grandmother set, and look how that turned out. Time is branching."

"Kellan will teach me how to navigate," Fawkes agreed. "Can we try again?"

Calisto nodded, satisfied. "When is Korsika going next?"

Fawkes implored the horizon with a hard squint, and his eyes swirled white. When he came back, he said, "I didn't see Korsika. I went to a random rainy day under the cedars, and I kept getting dripped on. I hate getting dripped on."

"At least you went misty this time. That's a step forward."

An earthquake ripped along the ground, making the air shiver, detonating Calisto's nerves. It was more intense than the one at Kellan's hut. And longer. Calisto closed their eyes and huddled on the ground, waiting for it to pass.

Fawkes's voice slashed through their attempt at deep breaths. "Calisto!"

They opened their eyes to find the cliff's edge crumbling and Fawkes scrabbling at vines. Calisto fought the disruption of the quake to reach for him. They grasped his arm as his feet plummeted down the rapidly decaying slope. Calisto's grip slipped.

But their hands knotted—and held.

The sun rolled sweat down Calisto's arm, flooding the palm that kept Fawkes from falling. The sea heaved with waves far below.

"I'm going to pull you up," Calisto said evenly.

Fawkes was light and Calisto was strong, but it took everything in their body to hoist him over the edge. They spun him away from the cliffs, and then momentum sent Calisto sailing. They fell right on top of him.

Calisto stared down into his gold-brown eyes. Fawkes's chest met theirs urgently when they breathed.

He was right here. With Calisto. Alive.

But this moment could have played out differently.

Calisto couldn't lose Fawkes when they'd just found each other. Korsika was branching the timelands *on purpose*, not caring about the lives he erased and destroyed in the process. Calisto felt the threat rattle along with the last of the quake. He had to be stopped.

"When is Korsika going?" Calisto asked in a hard whisper.

"Calisto . . ."

Their faces were so close together, and this time Calisto wasn't mostly asleep. They felt everything. The coarse fear as it left their body. The velvet warmth of Fawkes's skin. A moment that might become a kiss.

Destiny is just a choice you haven't made yet.

Before they could act on the choice they very much wanted to make, mist closed over Fawkes's eyes.

Calisto rolled away from him, dusted themself off, and resumed fashioning their own tunic until he returned.

"December 22, 1999," Fawkes said, lying on his back with his face to the sky, blinking with the intensity of a revelation.

"Why is Korsika going to that specific spot?"

"I have no idea! But I saw him there. Wearing a slightly too-small business suit and prowling around."

Fawkes smiled brilliantly and leapt to his feet, the almost-kiss forgotten.

Calisto had hoped they'd find a way back to that moment.

They sighed and looked out at the sea.

"You did it, Calisto! You anchored me! Why aren't you celebrating?" Fawkes rollicked up the path toward Kellan's hut, then came back and swept up Calisto in his delight. He pulled them to standing, kept hold of their hands, and stared straight into their eyes. Calisto felt his smile as strongly as the sun beating overhead.

"You help me stay here," he said, raising one hand and brushing his lips against the back of their knuckles. Calisto felt that tiny graze in unexpected places, shooting across their skin like falling stars. "From here we can go . . . anywhen."

His face lit with possibility. Fawkes tugged Calisto's hand, and they both danced all the way back to Kellan's hut.

THIRTEEN

Calisto and Fawkes stood on the beach in their tunics and time boots. They were ankle-deep in the surf, at Kellan's behest. "I just made this costume, and you want me to dunk it in the sea?" Calisto called to the shoreline, where Kellan paced.

"I'm delighted that you two figured out anchoring so quickly." They'd both run into the hut, breathless and brimming with discoveries. That was one of the lovelier parts of learning about time travel. Unfortunately, Kellan knew how quickly it could be overshadowed. "Now you must learn to travel with intention. Your clothing will be fine, *if* you time travel."

"Remember the Thames?" Fawkes said. "We went in that nasty water but came out in the mists dry."

"But if we *don't* travel, our costumes will be ruined," Calisto pointed out.

"Oh, they don't wear tunics in the nineties, outside of collegiate drunkenness. A strange vestige, that one. No, no. You are going to need flannel and distressed denim." Kellan tapped their forehead in concentration. "Korsika knows that era well. He'll have an advantage."

"Is it his hometime?" Fawkes asked.

"It is. And it's not a pretty one." Kellan grimaced, unwilling or unready to say more. "Korsika will know the way home. He might even bypass Pocket, as he's taken on some of Fawkes's ability. We have to hurry before his branching changes things beyond memory."

"Wait, go back," Fawkes said. "He can *keep* people's powers?"

"Not for long. Whatever he takes fades. So he just keeps taking. It's where he perfected the behavior." An unusually large wave slapped Kellan with cold, making them shiver-dance farther up the shore. "Let's start simple. You travel as a pair, but first, you must walk through the mists with confidence *alone*. Enter time by using one of the natural thresholds around you. Attempt to travel slightly forward from this point in time, but not space. If you can't, turn around and backtrack before you get immeasurably lost, and we never find you again."

As Kellan reached the end of their speech, Calisto ran for shore. Out of the folds of their mantle, they fished a spool of thread. "We can use this, like in the labyrinth. We'll pay it out as we walk through the mists and follow it back. *Safely.*"

Kellan clapped at the simple ingenuity of it. "Yes. Try that."

Calisto bit off two lengths of thread.

"Thank you," Fawkes said, receiving one solemnly.

"Begin!" Kellan cheered.

Calisto ran into the sea like someone who'd been taught to swim in a placid lake, as if the waves were personally out to get them. When a particularly big one came up, they dove under and disappeared.

Fawkes made his way delicately, pinching his lips against every wavelet. Kellan got the distinct impression that he didn't know how to swim, which made the Mediterranean as dangerous as the mists of time. Kellan got ready to play lifeguard as well as mentor. Fawkes pushed into the water up to his chin, then ducked under.

A few bubbles rose.

Kellan held their own breath.

Both travelers burst to the surface. Fawkes tossed his head and sent water in all directions, a prismatic explosion. Calisto glared at Kellan, undraping seaweed from their wrists and wringing water from their tunic.

"Any success?" Kellan asked, trying to keep a light, unbothered air. Pressure and fear wouldn't help these two find their way any faster.

"I spun around," Fawkes said. "I came out in a human-less era."

"I didn't go anywhen," Calisto said.

"Let's try a different approach." Kellan lined up Fawkes and Calisto at the mouth of a sea cave. The two ran toward the dark opening in a sort of race, dropping their threads behind them, sand spraying behind their heels and sticking to the oil-dark soles of their boots. They raced back out just as quickly.

"I went too far," Fawkes said. "*Way* too far. There were toilets all over the island."

"Nowhere, nowhen," Calisto said.

"Well." Kellan deflated. "That was a rousing disappointment. We won't give up."

Fawkes and Calisto disappeared over and over and came back again and again. The tide went out slowly. The sun slicked the horizon, and the sea blazed gold. Both pupils started to wilt with defeat.

Fawkes took off, wordlessly, up the beach. Calisto draped themself over a rock, arms and tunic splayed. "What am I doing *wrong*?"

"Nothing," Kellan said.

"Fine," Calisto said with a piercing look. "What else could I be doing *right*?"

Kellan smiled at the young traveler. "The first time I met you, you looked at me that way." They easily conjured the image of a grey-eyed baby with a stare like two straight pins.

"Were you the oracle who named me?" Calisto asked. "I wanted to ask before the quake happened."

"I am that oracle," Kellan said. "Your parents sought me out to help them find the path to . . . well . . . *you*."

"I know that part of the story. Tiye was pregnant with my sibling Myriad, and Nori wanted to have a baby with Tiye. They went to a clinic in the timelands."

"I located the right doctor for Nori. In return, your parents asked me to gift your name."

"So you're not just the reason I'm Calisto," they said. "You're the reason I *exist*?"

Kellan held up one clarifying finger. "I guide people, but I don't choose. Though our stories are more entwined than we know."

"Could you see my destiny when I was a baby?" Calisto asked.

"Only that we would meet again. It wasn't until later that I saw you traveling with Fawkes. When I learned *you're* the one who travels with direction."

"Me?" Calisto asked as they shot up to sitting. "If you know my time power, why are we doing this? Can't you tell me?"

"I'm afraid that if we don't come to certain things in our *own* time, they hold very little power at all."

Calisto groaned.

Kellan crouched among the tide pools. Little crabs scuttled sideways across the shallow bowl. "Power isn't an untouched and innate pool waiting inside you." They stirred the tide pool with a finger. "Power is in your perception. It is woven into the way you see things. This water is clear, but at sunset, it turns gold. Same pool, two different ways of perceiving it. Time is immaterial, and most people can't conceive of what is immaterial, so they see . . ."

"Nothing," Calisto said.

"Yes!" Kellan grinned. They were getting so desperate that every little step forward felt like a triumph. "They see a blankness, a mist, a void, a veritable vein of absence."

Calisto splashed their way to their feet. "I think you missed your calling as mystic poet. My siblings work at the wordhouse, if you change your mind."

A deep flush came over Kellan at the mention of the wordhouse. "Right. Well. What if you change how you see time, Calisto?"

"I'll try," they said, rallying. "If I can learn Mena's most demanding sewing techniques, I can learn this, too." They hiked their tunic up to their knees. They faced the beach bravely—then ran with force at an incoming wave, charging into a wall of water as it curled overhead.

The next wave tumbled them end over end and spat them out. They washed to shore like a half-dead fish, spitting seawater. Their thread had fallen from their hand and washed up, too.

"Anything?" Kellan shouted.

"Nothing," Calisto shouted back. "A blankness, a mist, a void." They spit salt. "A veritable vein of absence."

/// /// ///

Calisto sat on the hearth in Kellan's hut until their tunic dried out. Fawkes had curled up on the floor and gone to sleep in his uniquely abrupt way, and the oracle was sprawled on their straw pallet. Calisto poured themself another cup of twig-coffee.

They paced up and down the steep path that led to Kellan's hut. The stars were incredibly bright, nothing like in Pocket, where they shone through shifting patches of mist overhead. Here, they surrounded Calisto. Nearly swallowed them.

When they gave in to the fact that they wouldn't be sleeping, they sat under the light of those wild stars and sewed, thinking of Fawkes—and their moment on the cliffs. Its texture was different from any other moment they'd lived through. It asked to be touched. Fawkes's lips had hooked toward a smile, dusky pink and flushed. When he said their name in that thready, hopeful voice, it felt like . . .

Raw silk.

Calisto ran up the hill, yelling, "Kellan! Wake up! I have an idea!"

Before they reached the hut, another quake took hold. Calisto staggered up the path. Everything felt wrong—inside and out. Starlight blurred as reality shuddered. Calisto could barely put one time boot in front of another. "Fawkes! Kellan!"

Both emerged just before the hut collapsed, beams snapping like rickety old bones.

"Stand clear!" Kellan pulled Fawkes to safety.

The jagged feeling wore on and on. The quake lasted for interminable moments.

When the universe resettled, Kellan's hut was a heap of crumbled walls and broken pottery. The oracle stared at the ruins like they were a surprise, which caught Calisto sideways. Even oracles could be blindsided.

"Kellan, I'm sorry about your hut."

"We were lucky it was just my home and not the subatomic structure of our bodies. I suppose that's coming next."

"What do you mean?" Fawkes asked.

Kellan poked the wreckage with a foot. "Branching this strong will send vibrations across the timelands. Vibrations can be quite dangerous to life. When space programs develop rocket ships, they know there's a real chance that unprecedented vibrations could turn astronauts into atomic soup. They do it anyway."

"Is that meant to be an encouraging story?" Calisto asked. "Is there any way to stop this?"

"We need to catch up to Korsika as quickly as we can," Fawkes worked out. "Time has to settle, or we could get rattled out of existence."

"Just like an Etch A Sketch," Kellan mumbled grimly before shaking their head. "I'm afraid you two need to push on from Crete while there's a chance to tip the course of time in a better direction. Now, you have an idea that you wanted to share with me, Calisto?" Kellan clearly wanted to look encouraging but mostly looked desperate.

"I figured something out," Calisto said. "I need my tailor's outfit."

They pointed to the rubble that used to be Kellan's hut. Fawkes moved nimbly over the remains. Calisto joined in from the sidelines of the wreckage, sifting and pulling out Kellan's possessions one by one. The pottery was all smashed, of course. But the dented kettle was intact.

"I found our things," Fawkes cried, pulling Calisto's cloak free and waving it like a flag. "Don't worry, it's all here."

He appeared at their side with the bag Calisto had made, stuffed with the surviving costume pieces. They went down to the beach, and Calisto changed into their tailor's outfit in a sea cave. When they emerged, Calisto switched places with Fawkes, giving him strict instructions to put on the best twentieth-century costume pieces he could muster and not to mix them up with others.

Kellan waited on the shoreline, studying the sea foam. Calisto approached. For the first time since the two had met, the oracle's solitude looked properly *lonely*.

"I have a costume for you." Calisto reached into the bag and took out what they'd been sewing earlier. It was the minotaur's pelt, reworked with tight, neat stitches invisible to the eye. "So you can look like a true monster when you need to."

"Calisto!" Kellan said, a few grateful tears prickling their face. "Are you sure you're ready to take the next steps?"

"No," they said. "But I realized how I see time, and it isn't immaterial. It's the opposite, in fact. So thank you for . . . well, not *showing* me but helping me fail so spectacularly that I figured it out myself."

"Teaching isn't a linear art," Kellan said. "If you need a trial run—"

"We're out of luck. You said it yourself. That quake was ten times bigger than the first. Besides, I can't let Korsika go around selling time boots to anyone rich or greedy enough to buy a pair. Pocket would be overrun, and I'd never forgive myself." As they'd seen Mena do so many times before, they warded themself against the evil eye and spat.

Fawkes emerged from the sea cave wearing his shalwar trousers and vest—nothing under it—and securing the silk tie around his head. "What is that doing up there?" Calisto asked, pointing.

"Don't they wear sweatbands?"

"You're thinking of the eighties," Kellan mooned.

"I was close!" Fawkes crowed, as if missing by one era counted as a victory.

"This will have to do for traveling," Calisto said. "We'll figure out new costumes once we get there."

"When we're headed, shopping malls are plentiful and terrifying," Fawkes promised.

Calisto shivered. "Mena would never speak to me if I wore something from a *mall.*"

"I hate to tell you this," Kellan said, "but if you want to blend in when you're going, that's exactly what you'll need to do. Which is one of the *many* reasons I didn't settle down in that wasteland of an era."

"Is it dangerous?" Calisto asked.

"Yes," Kellan said. "But for people like us, the dangers never die—they shapeshift. You'll face them in many forms. You'll feel brave sometimes, and less brave others. But you'll be together."

Fawkes flew at Kellan and gave them a brief but intense hug, and then ran into the shallows, kicking at small waves with his time boots. "Are we going?" he asked, a tug in his tone, always so ready to leave.

Calisto thanked the oracle of Knossos.

They held out one hand to Fawkes, and together they walked into the waves of the dark organza sea.

FOURTEEN

The first time Mena took Calisto into the back room of the costume shop, they'd been overwhelmed by material. In one cupboard: crepe, cashmere, and canvas. Linen, leather, lawn. Frothed lace in so many patterns. Muslin. Gingham. Georgette. Jersey. A thicket of plaids. Silk and suede and taffeta, tulle, twill, and tweed. The short pile of velvets and velours. Beyond that cupboard: so many others. A richness of possibility—little Calisto had stared, unsure of where to begin.

They felt the same way inside of time. But they knew what to look for. Instead of letting the whiteness drift by like incorporeal mist, they found another shifting, unrolling, reality.

Fabric.

Calisto had pinched the stuff of time between their fingers once—you couldn't do that with mist—and drawn it apart like a curtain. It was pearlescent and light, sheer and overlapping. If the moment when Calisto and Fawkes almost kissed was raw silk, this was chiffon.

They took a few steps, reached out, and touched a single point in the fabric of time.

It rippled through them. Crete, again, but later. Kellan was walking along the line of the surf.

Calisto took another step, touched another point. This was Crete, too, but after an earthquake and tsunami had flayed open the cities, tore down the pillars and palaces, ate at the cliffs, and remapped the shores.

Calisto gasped. It was so *tangible*.

"I can feel exactly when we are," Calisto said.

If they were going to the late 1990s, they couldn't do it a few steps at a time like this, sliding their fingers down the fabric. It would take forever, and, besides, feeling moments with such immediacy was an incredible experience.

Feeling more than two millennia of moments would swamp a person easily.

Calisto did what Mena had taught them to do. They took pins from their trouser pockets, a needle, and thread. Black this time, to stand out against the shifting white. They stuck the pins in their mouth.

"We're about to move quickly," Calisto said as they threaded the needle. "Hold on to me, Fawkes."

Without question or hesitation, Fawkes's hand tightened on their arm. "My turn to keep you anchored." Calisto nodded thanks. With his help, they would stay grounded and not lose track of themself as they faced the enormity of existence.

They began to sew.

The fabric of time was supple but slippery. Finding a rhythm with their needle took some work. They used basting stitches, quick and simple, impermanent. They weren't leaving a lasting mark but sketching a map to where they needed to be. Instead of perfection, they aimed for speed, moving down the eras, each so defined by popular expression. They grew faster, more confident. Fabric flew under their fingertips. Fawkes kept up, barely.

Calisto paused to let their fingers brush, checking where and when they were. The Middle Ages in Europe, everyone in sackcloth. There was still so much farther to go. They stitched a little faster.

They brushed the fabric again and found they'd moved in space—which was woven together with time, like a fabric's warp and weft—to North Africa in the 1700s, electric with trade, the rich yellows and reds of Moroccan hand dyes lingering in Calisto's sight as they kept stitching.

The 1800s flashed by. Calisto brushed against England's Victorian era, stiff with starch. The 1900s arrived. Calisto felt the moment when the homespun clothes of the early century gave way to store-bought, then mass-produced. Here were the wildly bright and wholly synthetic styles of the 1970s and 1980s. For a brief moment, everything flashed neon.

They were getting close.

In the 1990s, style split—dark suits in one direction, shredded denim in the other.

The millennium beckoned, just ahead.

Calisto stopped short: 1999.

"I've got the year!" Calisto said. "But how do I know we're in the right place?"

"Korsika was at his old school. A place called Stanford."

Calisto knew about Stanford, thanks to Richard and his academics. It was in California. Calisto moved across the weave of the fabric. They touched a new point—and found themself looking at jeweled fjords in Norway.

"Wrong way."

They ripped out those stitches with their teeth, backtracking to the place where they'd gone wrong. Then they headed across the weave in the other direction. Over the Atlantic. Across the East Coast of what was now the United States, brushing briefly on New England with its preppy styles, the Midwest and its buttoned-up ways.

Calisto landed right where they needed to be: Northern California, a stitch before the turn of the millennium. There was a bright, sunny ripple to the fabric. They felt their way around the San Francisco Bay with its safety-pin punks, its fiercely plumed drag queens, over to a more muted suburban spot. Palo Alto.

They gave themself a moment to marvel. "I found it."

"Calisto, you're a time tailor." Fawkes's voice was edged with bright wonder. "I should have known!"

"That's all right, Fawkes. I found it when I was ready."

Calisto removed a pin from their mouth, took a breath, and stuck it deep into the fabric.

The 1990s in suburban California greeted them with a fresh blast of green—trees and lawns laid out geometrically, vivid but controlled compared to Crete's feral edges. Basketball nets stood tall in driveways next to identical one-story houses. Droop-necked streetlamps lined the sidewalks. Bright yellow stitches ran along the center of pitch-colored streets.

They'd landed on one of those streets, a mostly quiet one, but when cars came, they whizzed by at alarming speeds. Fawkes had to pull Calisto out of the way of a minivan right before it clipped them. "Don't they stop for people?"

"Have you never seen a car before?" Fawkes asked.

"I've heard about them," Calisto said, as if they were legendary monsters about as likely as minotaurs.

"Let me lead the way," Fawkes said. "Staying safe in modern eras requires absurd skills that I have been hoarding my whole life."

Calisto nodded, more than willing to let Fawkes be the one who understood this bizarre place.

They both set off down the sidewalk, the December sun weak but warm enough that Calisto could take off their many-scrap cloak and wear it around their waist like the sleeve-tied sweatshirts and flannels they saw all around.

When they reached a stretch of restaurants and shops, Fawkes pulled Calisto into one with thrilled urgency. There were humming machines stacked along every wall, people grumbling as they tossed in clothes and coins. It smelled of bracing soap and the residue of bad decisions.

"What is this place?" Calisto asked.

"A time traveler's best friend," Fawkes said. "A *laundromat*."

They sat and watched through bubbled windows as clothes spun and spun. Calisto found it mesmerizing, one machine battering the garments clean, another battering them dry. Whenever a buzzing timer went off, Calisto jumped. Fawkes paid hawklike attention. One of the dryers stopped, and nobody stepped up to claim the warm heap of fabric.

Fawkes dove in and came back clutching fistfuls of denim and flannel like the spoils of battle. "Can you use this?"

"It's *perfection*." Calisto side-hugged Fawkes so hard that he tipped over a little. He bobbed back up, looking proud. "We should leave something in return. And I don't think they use moon coins here."

"I'm out of extra time boots," Fawkes said in all seriousness.

Calisto shook their head and grabbed the clothes. They left behind a few swatches of fabric from their tailor's stash—bright silk from the Steppes, the quality so high it should fetch a good price in any era.

Moments later, Fawkes and Calisto barricaded themselves in a public bathroom in a nearby coffee shop. Calisto assembled a costume: cut-off jean shorts and black tights shredded with ladder runs. They kept their belt lined with sharp tailoring tools. They layered a black tank top with their magenta waistcoat, tied a flannel around their waist, wore another as an overshirt, and slung yet a third flannel around their shoulders like a half cape.

"Is that the right amount of shirts?" Fawkes asked when they came out of the bathroom stall.

"Flannel is *very* popular in the 1990s," Calisto said authoritatively. "I don't think we can wear too much. What about your shirt?" Fawkes wore ripped jeans and a white T-shirt that he'd scrawled on with a Sharpie he'd borrowed from a barista writing names on cups.

It said ASK ME HOW I TIME TRAVEL.

"Every third person we pass is wearing a wordy shirt," Fawkes said. "And the best camouflage doesn't *hide* who you are—it just keeps you from getting eaten."

"Hmmm." Calisto was unfortunately charmed by this shirt that would draw attention to their presence. "Fine. One more thing." They fished out the charcoal pencil from their tailor's stash and held it up to Fawkes's face.

"Are you going to stick that in my eye?" he yelped, stepping back and hitting the sink.

"It's goes *around* your eye," Calisto said, pencil still leveled. "Trust me."

Calisto steadied his face with one hand, aiming the dark pencil with the other. Focused on the dip of every lash, the landscape of his face became strange again, fascinating in a whole new way. His eyes stayed gently closed as Calisto ran the pencil back and forth. He had a light smile on his lips. His hands curled and uncurled with nervous energy.

Calisto wanted to kiss him.

Calisto *was going* to kiss him.

Fawkes's eyes shot open. They went vague and misty. A few moments later, he came back with a blink.

"That's happened twice *right* when I was about to kiss you!" Calisto said, unable to keep the truth in any longer. Fawkes blushed so hard that Calisto had a horrible, wonderful, instantaneous understanding of what had happened. "Did I anchor you again? Did you mind-walk right into us kissing?"

"Yes." He blinked faster, thrown into panic mode. "It only started coming up since we've been traveling together . . ."

Calisto tucked away the charcoal pencil. "Will you tell me about kissing visions when they happen? It's only fair for me to know, too." They could feel a smile on their own lips, warmth running rampant through their chest. They were starting to enjoy talking about this. Anticipating it.

"Are you sure?"

"I think so." Calisto sat on the edge of the sink, facing Fawkes. "I'm new to having a nonlinear relationship."

"Ha," Fawkes said. "I'm old hat at it. What *is* that saying? You know, about hats. What about having experience makes someone an old one?"

"I have no idea," Calisto said. "So, kissing. When were we doing it? What did it feel like?"

"Right," Fawkes said. "It's hard to say when it was. I was a little too busy. And the whole moment was *us*. The bigger picture was blotted out by this feeling that makes things go hazy. Moments stretch out longer than they should be able to. Have you felt that?"

Calisto had not.

"You closed your eyes, and then I closed my eyes, and everything went warm and rushed at me, and I felt my edges, and I was also . . . dissolving into brightness." Calisto's breath snagged. "I thought traveling together was the best thing I'd felt, and then I felt *this*."

Fawkes twisted and twisted a single curl, his nervous thinking habit activated.

Calisto reached out and twirled the strand for him, then let their fingers drift through his dark hair. Fawkes closed his eyes against the feeling, leaning into Calisto's hand. A low, untamed hum rose from deep in his throat.

Calisto leaned in close.

Fawkes leaned in closer.

Someone banged on the door of the tiny room.

Calisto startled out of the dreamy atmosphere, hitting reality a bit too hard. Fawkes bit his lip and pulled his hands back like he'd touched a hot stove.

"We should go out there," Calisto said as the person outside banged again and threatened to tell the management.

"Wait. How do I look?" Fawkes asked.

Calisto pulled back to admire their work. Fawkes's eyes were darkly lined and glowing. "You know I like how you look."

Fawkes gifted them with the very best smile.

Back in the coffee shop, Calisto hunted for a baggy, single-pocket sweatshirt with the word STANFORD emblazoned on it. They found one on a student grasping an enormous mocha. Some costumes gave subtle hints about where and when a person hailed from—others were as simple as signposts.

Calisto charged forward, forgetting the part about Fawkes taking the lead. To be fair, he seemed a little turned around by what had happened in the bathroom.

"We need to get back to campus, but we got lost," Calisto said in English vaguely accented by Seam, a language that nobody here spoke or even knew about. "Can you point us back?"

"Sure," the Stanford student said a little warily. If there was something out of place about Fawkes and Calisto, they didn't look off-putting enough to keep the student from pointing directions to the campus a few blocks away.

They strolled green lawns, past beige stone towers and the long arcade of the fancy school. Calisto inspected the students. Bootcut jeans, polos, more Stanford apparel. A few artfully baggy outfits or jackets covered in fascinating patches, but those were deeply outnumbered by basic cotton T-shirts that inscrutably bore the word GAP. A small flock went by in pajama bottoms and flip-flops on their way to a large building that exuded the smell of sickly sweet waffles.

"We still look . . . different," Calisto said.

Fawkes cocked his head. "We *are* different."

Calisto had always been proud of the things that made them stand out—in Pocket. They'd been taught that in the timelands, difference was a constant source of danger. Maybe that was true. But maybe, sometimes, costumes for time travelers could be about more than keeping the wolves at bay. Calisto decided to bring this up with Mena when they got home.

When they *both* got home.

Which was starting to feel farther and farther away.

Fawkes ducked into one of the dormitory buildings and came back with a thick student directory. Calisto looked through the list of names and buildings and rooms. The vast majority of dorm bedrooms were shared. After a quick search, they found not one but *two* familiar names.

Omen Korsika. Kellan Herrera.

"Well, that explains why Kellan didn't sound surprised by Korsika choosing the nineties," Calisto said.

"Why didn't Kellan tell us they know him?" Fawkes asked, looking mildly betrayed.

"Would you?"

"If someone asked me, I would," Fawkes said. "But otherwise . . . no. Why do you think Korsika came here?"

"There must be something he's trying to change by giving himself the time-boot formula during this era. Otherwise, why be so specific?"

Calisto and Fawkes made their way across campus. This was a planned, pruned, and parceled-out environment—designed to be simple for students to navigate—so it wasn't hard to track down the building they were looking for.

"What do we do when we find Korsika?" Calisto asked as they headed up four flights of stairs.

"We stop him," Fawkes said.

"Right," Calisto said. "And how do we stop him?"

"Kellan didn't cover that part, did they?"

"The quakes cut our lessons short." They reached the landing and looked at identical doors until they found one with a whiteboard that bore Kellan's and Korsika's names, scribbled in different hands. Kellan's looped to the point it was nearly illegible. Korsika's was written in a bold, all-caps style.

Calisto and Fawkes put their ears to the door but could only hear muffled, indistinct voices.

"What now?" Calisto asked.

Fawkes rapped at the door without warning. Calisto jumped back.

"Yeah? Come in." It was Kellan's voice, but even brighter if that were possible, stripped of age.

Fawkes opened the door just a crack and said, "Hey, I was looking for Omen."

"Yeah, he's not here at this exact moment!"

"Sorry to interrupt you."

"Not to worry." The second voice also sounded familiar to Calisto. It had a light, crisp quality, an unmistakable Scottish burr. "Do you want us to tell him you dropped by?"

"Nope," Fawkes said, "I really don't want that."

He drew back but left the door open a hair.

Calisto was impressed.

They pressed up to the thin crack. Kellan sat on a narrow bed with someone Calisto had never seen, or even imagined, outside of Pocket. "That's Dr. Gillian Jacobs," Calisto whispered. "She runs the wordhouse. She's in the Loose Association and Book Club of Elders. When she's older, I mean."

"Huh," Fawkes said. "The backstory thickens."

Calisto took in the sight of young Gillian in a jean skirt and white button-down, her red hair swept up with a chewed pen. Kellan looked angular in cargo pants and a T-shirt that read THE TRUTH IS OUT THERE.

"See?" Fawkes mouthed silently. "Wordy shirt!"

"We have to figure this out before Omen gets back," Kellan said.

"Why in the world would you show him your time boots?" Gillian asked. "He's not a natural traveler. It's only going to make him wild, wanting to follow us."

Kellan swallowed. "Korsika and I are . . . we've gotten closer."

"Closer than roommates?" Gillian asked in mock confusion. "Yes, I've noticed."

Fawkes mouthed to Calisto, *"What?"*

Calisto shrugged.

Kellan had seemed awfully alone on Crete, in that tiny hut. Calisto wasn't shocked to find out that the oracle had romantic entanglements with other travelers. *Which* travelers made a few more pieces of the temporal puzzle fall into place.

No wonder Kellan wanted to stop Korsika so badly: they felt somewhat responsible.

"I thought we weren't doing jealousy," Kellan said, flopping a worried hand through their hair.

"We're not. It's just . . . *Omen.*"

Calisto choked on a laugh.

"Is somebody in the hallway?" Gillian asked, but Kellan was standing up and forging ahead with the conversation.

"I thought you liked him, too!"

"I did. In case you've forgotten, I was the one who kissed him at the Halloween party. We dated for two months, and then he wanted to sell one of my ideas as base code for all-language translation tech."

"Everyone is selling ideas to Silicon Valley right now," Kellan said with a shrug. "They all want to . . . ruffle the feathers of the future! Korsika thought he was helping you do that. I think?"

"And I think he's an entitled nightmare capitalist dingo baby."

"Now, that's simply word salad."

"I'm *almost* a linguist, and I think it describes Korsika perfectly."

"Speaking of linguistics, have you been working on those temporal words?" Kellan asked.

"I need more practice." Gillian sighed. "I swear I'm close to getting them to *work*, but it's one thing to know that a word has power, and another to try to use that power to change the flow of time, even extremely locally." Calisto wondered what that meant, and if it was Gillian's time power. None of their siblings at the wordhouse had ever mentioned it. "I can't focus on temporal words if I'm worried about Omen and . . . whatever Omen is trying to get out of you for his own gain."

Kellan slid onto the bed beside Gillian. "He wants to be a traveler. Think about the night when we showed him my mind-walking and how you can keep me anchored. He anchored me, too, Gillian! He was impressive, really! How can you explain that if he has no natural aptitude? When he asked me where I'd been over Thanksgiving break, I couldn't help it. The rest fell out."

"And you're sure he *believed* that you went back to Tenochtitlán?"

At that moment, Omen Korsika—a young version with the same baggy sweatpants and haughty demeanor—appeared at the end of the hall. Fawkes and Calisto dove onto anemic couches in the adjoining lounge. Calisto picked up a magazine to peer over. Fawkes studied his reflection in a bulbous brass lamp.

Omen's T-shirt matched the style of Kellan's, only this version read TRUST NO ONE.

He stuck his head into the room he shared with Kellan. "Am I interrupting something?"

"Yes," Gillian said.

"No," Kellan said brightly.

"I thought we should talk. About . . . our mutual interest."

"We are not doing this now." Gillian shut him down as swiftly as he'd arrived.

"Okay." Omen drummed his fingers on the doorframe. "Later?"

"Tonight," Kellan promised as they gently closed the door. "At the party."

Omen left the hall, and Calisto and Fawkes followed him at a safe distance. He went to a physics lecture and sulked through a lunch of french fries at the dining hall. By the time he started playing Hacky Sack on the green, things were looking dire. And not just because a solitary game of Hacky Sack was one of the saddest things Calisto had ever seen.

"There's no sign of Korsika's older self," Calisto said. "Did we miss him?"

"There would have been more branching quakes if he made whatever move he's planning in this era." Fawkes leaned against one of the manicured trees on the green. "He could be waiting to make his entrance."

Omen caught the Hacky Sack on the side of his foot. It trembled there, then dropped to the ground.

"You don't think *that* was the big moment he came for?" Calisto asked.

"Based on what he did at the Globe, I'd say he wants something grander."

Calisto's mind caught on something Kellan had said in the dorm. "Like . . . a party?"

FIFTEEN

Korsika limped toward the club on his stabbed foot.

He had arrived in 1999 well before the party began. He relished his hometime now that he was no longer tied down to it. Eucalyptus filled the air, making it balmy to the touch. The asphalt of identical cul-de-sacs was infused with constant sun. Stanford had stocked its campus with fresh-faced, newly hatched adults who believed they could mold the future with their unfettered dreams and great talents.

This moment tasted of *hope*. A sense that things could only get better. That progress was tantalizingly possible, and anyone who resisted it would be swept out of the way. Korsika had bought into it fully. But the start-ups would only be offering a smarter phone, a faster internet connection, some technological bauble that would at best distract people, and in many cases make things worse as eras flew past.

That was about to change. He was walking—limping—through his past with the formula for a truly different future.

The time savant had shown him exactly when to deliver it.

He'd hardly enjoyed chasing Fawkes through the mists instead of asking Kellan for help. But Kellan was lost to him. At least in this go-round. He'd ruined too much, and it was time for the great reset that would make it all right.

He arrived at Club Capacitor, a box of dark glass that had seemed thrilling in his youth and now looked a bit squalid. And yet here was the crux he'd been looking for: in his life, in the timeline. It had to be this night. Of course it did. He felt silly that he hadn't thought of it sooner.

Korsika touched his pocket, checking the formula he'd written down after locating it in the old cobbler's head. His own calculations for making time boots had been so close to complete, and there was hardly glory in abandoning them. But the Time Wardens had figured out what he was planning, and they'd come after him with a fearful speed.

He wouldn't be detained—and he wouldn't lose this chance.

Not after so much work. Not after so much *hope*.

He was admitted to the club by a squirrelly bouncer who gave him a bit of a glare but didn't ask for an ID. Korsika was too old to be carded. He set himself up in a corner, trying not to look ancient or overdressed for a night at a campus haunt. He'd arrived in California in doublet and hose, so he'd ducked into a dry cleaner and pretended he was an actor with a lost ticket stub, eyeballing sizes as best he could.

This uninspired grey suit that cut off well above his ankles was better than the doublet but not quite right for this crowd. Or for meeting his destiny.

Here it was, entering the club in the form of his younger self.

Korsika had to admit that young Omen wasn't dressed finely, either. He wore what he'd considered his uniform back then: grey sweatpants, a loose denim shirt, a cleverish T-shirt. And was that . . . oh, dear. Korsika had conveniently forgotten his youthful penchant for hemp necklaces.

Kellan and Gillian were late. Probably off somewhere talking about him, laughing together, trying to decide his fate. Korsika would have to wait for them. They were important factors in this equation. He knew what was going to happen next. He knew everything about this night, down to the smallest detail. He'd never been able to stop reliving it.

A quake ripped through the club, nearly knocking him to his knees. He reached out to steady himself as his drink shivered out of his hand, hit the dirty dance floor, and smashed.

"Well, *that* was different," he muttered.

The quake subsided, and people in the bar shrugged it off.

Outside on the streets of Palo Alto, Fawkes and Calisto were the only ones who seemed to care about the shaking. After a few quick and mostly drunken shouts, people turned back to obsessing over a different worry.

"Why is everyone talking about something called Y2K?" Calisto asked as they followed a stream of people—including Kellan and Gillian—past houses plastered with Greek symbols to the city beyond.

"It's a theoretical computer malfunction that aligns with a big calendar change," Fawkes said.

"They think that's scarier than everything quaking?"

"There's a fault line here, so people are probably used to a certain amount of quaking. They think the millennium is a bigger deal because it only comes around every thousand years. People in the timelands create things like ages and centuries and millennia, and then get twitchy about them." Fawkes wanted to tap on some shoulders and politely inform these partygoers that they weren't quite being original. "Humans love to celebrate when they think the world is ending. Have you met Vikings who think Ragnarok is about to start? Fin-de-siècle soirees have glorious music and tons of champagne. Oh, and in the postpocalypse, there are these bonfires, some as tall as buildings, and everyone burns their old stuff and dances naked."

"Have you met those Vikings and drunk that champagne and danced naked around those particular bonfires?" Calisto asked.

"I'm a bit of a magnet for end-times."

"That's a very specific form of bad luck," Calisto said.

"I know." Fawkes grabbed their hand and pulled them into the line outside of a club. Kellan and Gillian were waiting to get in a few steps ahead. "I didn't land in those eras on purpose, but when in Rome . . . Well, I've *been* to Rome, and their end-of-civilization parties were orgies and throwing slaves at lions—I skipped those."

Kellan and Gillian entered the club, and the line moved forward a few paces. "Since you've been to so many parties, you can help me with this one. Not the apocalypse parts. I've never been to a dance except moonful festivals, or when Ndeye and Massamba have parties in their garden, or Ells hosts a barn dance, and I'm discovering how uneventful my life sounds as I say this out loud."

When Fawkes and Calisto reached the head of the line, the bouncer stared expectantly.

"What does this person want?" Calisto whispered.

"Proof of our age on a little plastic card," Fawkes whispered in return.

"Why?"

"Because this is a club where people drink and cavort and do things that require forethought. This era has no true metric for wisdom, so they've chosen a random number."

"IDs," the bouncer barked.

"We're exchange students," Fawkes announced. "We don't have driver's licenses."

To Calisto, he added in a swift undertone: "I tried to drive a car once. It did *not* go well."

"No IDs, no drinks," the bouncer said, inking their hands with a neon skull stamp and waving them through.

Fawkes twined an arm through Calisto's. Together, they moved into the smoky innards of the club. Fawkes spat out chemical fog as Calisto shed one of their many flannels in the wave of body heat. People flooded toward the bar.

"Do you see them?" Calisto asked.

"Not yet."

They plunged deeper into the overcrowded darkness. Fawkes hated gatherings like this. People on all sides. The loveliness of music peeled away until it was just noise and bone-thump. Everyone trying to spin desperate meaning out of time because they thought it might be running out.

Calisto's body snagged on the aggressive beat. Fawkes watched as they scanned the room, swaying listlessly, arms moving like seaweed on a weak tide.

"Are you dancing?" Fawkes asked.

"I don't know how it works here."

Fawkes might not have been in his element, but Calisto looked truly lost. He put his hands on their hips.

Calisto's eyes widened.

Fawkes's fingers fanned out as he gently nudged Calisto in the direction of the beat. When they found it, their bodies slid into an easier alignment. Calisto's hands seemed unsure of themselves though. In not knowing where to go, they took such a journey: up Fawkes's arms and down his shoulders like soft rain, and then with their palms flat over his chest, where they must have encountered his heart beating *so quickly.*

None of this looked quite how the other people around them were dancing, but Fawkes did not care. Something in the two of their bodies had been fused together by the beat of this otherwise awful music. Calisto's hands slid up Fawkes's shoulders and knotted loosely behind his neck, which only brought them closer together as they rocked their hips. A stream of unbelievable energy moved through Fawkes, a current flowing between them.

Calisto tugged at a curl on the back of Fawkes's neck, and he thought he might die. Not a bad sort of dying.

"That's, um, that's a good spot for your hands," Fawkes mumbled. "Accurate to the time period."

"Have you danced this way with people in those end-times we talked about?" Calisto was shouting over the music, and yet no one else could hear them. Which made it feel like Calisto and Fawkes were in their own small slice of world. "I've danced with my friends at festivals but not like this."

"I've tried some things out." Fawkes shrugged and felt Calisto's fingertips resting softly on his neck. "To see what they felt like."

"What did they feel like?"

"Also not this."

A smile darted over Calisto's lips. "Are we cavorting?"

Their delight faded before Fawkes could answer. "There he is!" Calisto shouted into Fawkes's ear. "Well, *young* him."

"Where?" Fawkes asked as Calisto pulled away. Thoughts of dancing scattered, but the sensation lingered, a sort of sweet painful echo.

Calisto pointed toward the small stage, where the DJ was doing . . . whatever DJs did. "Omen doesn't look like he's enjoying himself."

Omen was, in fact, languishing by the speakers. He caught sight of young Kellan and Gillian by the bar, getting drinks for all three of them, and the grey clouds of his sulking lifted.

He'd clearly missed the sight of his older self in the far corner of the room.

Fawkes found Korsika looming there, shrouded by acrid-smelling fog that poured forth from a machine. Laser beams punctured the foggy darkness, and so did the DJ who kept shouting, "Welcome to the future!!!"

Korsika spotted Fawkes and Calisto across the room, eyes piercing like more of those awful lasers.

"Korsika knows we're here." Calisto grasped Fawkes's arm. "We have to cut him off before he gets to his younger self."

"Or Time Wardens show up and crash the party," Fawkes added.

Together, Fawkes and Calisto took a step forward.

Fawkes faltered.

Calisto knew what was going wrong even before the mists fell over Fawkes's eyes. They tugged at his arm, but it was too late. Tremors ran rampant through his body. One hand rose to his temple and smashed it, over and over, as if to jar what he was seeing out of his head.

Calisto pried his hand away so he couldn't keep hitting himself.

Fawkes's arm went limp.

"So this is terrifying," Calisto muttered. They tried to stay calm and anchor him, instead of letting him be tossed by inner winds. "This moment needs you, Fawkes," they said in a low, even voice. "I need you here with me."

Fawkes's head twitched in their direction.

"Can you hear me? It's Calisto. We're Fawkes and Calisto. We're supposed to do this *together*."

Calisto needed his gold-brown eyes to blink away the mist. But Fawkes stayed lost in what he was seeing, what he was *living*.

Meanwhile, Korsika moved toward his younger self.

Calisto couldn't miss this part.

They tugged Fawkes to the wall and propped him up. It felt wrong to abandon him, but the other option was to forget why they'd come all this way in the first place. Calisto ran across the club, blocking Korsika's path to . . . himself.

"Hey!" Calisto got in the older traveler's way. "We're not letting you do this."

"We?" Korsika asked almost whimsically, looking around and locating Fawkes. "The time savant seems to be elsewhen at the moment." He mocked up a frown. "I remember how inconvenient that could be for Kellan."

"*Kellan* sent us here to stop you," Calisto said.

Korsika wavered, looking at the young version of the oracle loading up on drinks at the bar. "How did they propose you do that? Kellan's an idealist. They don't think things through. You don't have any way to stop me, do you?" Calisto deeply disliked how much this argument echoed their own thoughts. "Stabbing my foot in this club isn't going to play out well. The police in this era are quite overzealous."

Across the room, Kellan and Gillian caught up to Omen, handing over a drink from their bounty of cups.

Korsika sighed. "Congratulations, you've delayed the inevitable." He fished out the formula for time boots from the pocket of his painfully standard suit. "I have to wait for another opportunity to give myself the blueprint to a better future. For everyone."

"You stole that, like you steal everything. And you're not here to become the magnificent inventor of time boots. I know why you're here," Calisto said. "Your sweatpants told me everything."

"Ah, yes," Korsika said. "The sweatpants augury again."

"When I met you at the shop, you were wearing basically the same clothes as you are in 1999. You've been stuck here! That's why you came back. Giving people time boots is a way to make yourself feel better about whatever went wrong."

Korsika's wry expression collapsed. His amused tolerance for Calisto ran out.

Fawkes leapt into belated action and rushed across the club, launching himself onto Korsika's back.

"Fawkes!" Calisto cried.

"Help me get him out!" Fawkes said. "The people here think they're civilized. They'll tell us to—"

"Leave!" the bartender shouted as Korsika flung him off. "You three! Out!"

"Well, it worked," Fawkes said in a crumpled tone as Calisto scraped him off the floor.

"What are you *doing*?" they asked.

"Buying us time."

The bouncer escorted all three of them out of the bar. Kellan,

Gillian, and Omen gave the disruption a momentary glance, but their attention didn't stick. They went back to drinking and talking in a huddle.

In the alley behind the bar, as soon as the bouncer vanished, Korsika whirled on Fawkes and Calisto. "Tell me one thing. Why do you believe *you're* the ones who deserve time travel?" His easy smile and charm had been whisked away. "Because it's the birthright of being born in a particular valley? Because you accidentally stumbled onto it when you were a child? This should be available to all of humanity, not a special, secret few. It's so incredibly *selfish* of you to keep it to yourselves."

"What you're doing is unselfish?" Calisto asked. "Who benefits from selling time boots?"

"And who suffers?" Fawkes asked. "I saw everything that will happen if you give yourself that formula."

"Wait," Calisto said. "How?"

"The branch is so close to becoming reality. I could feel how far it will fracture."

So *that's* what Fawkes had seen in the club.

Korsika watched him, eyes screwed up, face unreadable.

"Pocket will be overrun, destroyed," Fawkes said. "People will travel without any sense of how or why. For every new traveler, new Time Wardens will oppose them. They'll fight, crossing the mists and the timelands and churning them like the mud of any battlefield. Reality will rip itself apart." Fawkes blinked and refocused on Korsika, shaking off the air of prophecy. "You're about to start a completely avoidable apocalypse. Did you feel the quake earlier? It's starting."

"What a cheap trick," Korsika said with a blustering laugh. "Is that all Kellan wanted you to do? Chant doomsday messages at me? I don't believe a word."

"Then why are you still standing here?" Calisto asked.

Korsika's smugness returned in full force. "You happened to put me precisely where I want to be. All I had to do was wait."

Kellan, Gillian, and Omen came out of the bar, laughing. They were so wrapped up in one another—in their shared moment—that they didn't notice they were being watched.

"You're going to love this." Kellan kissed Omen on the corner of his lips. "I'll be right back."

Omen looked dizzyingly happy.

"Behold!" Kellan said. "Time travel!"

Gillian and Kellan linked arms and traipsed off into the night's thick fog.

They walked into time together, leaving Omen alone.

"Kellan? Gillian?" His face folded furiously. "Come back!"

Calisto saw the aftermath unspool. Omen didn't want to be left behind. He didn't understand time as easily as his friends did, and even his time power was based in taking from other travelers. If he "discovered" the secret behind time boots, though, he would feel important again.

He would change this story, and that would change everything.

Calisto grabbed Korsika before he could walk up to young, lonely Omen.

Korsika spun. His hand closed around Calisto's wrist like a tourniquet. Everything went black. They fell to the ground, hands twitching as if they were sewing, sewing, sewing, at top speed.

154

"That's a lovely ability," Korsika said. "Thank you." He left them in a flannel-covered heap.

Fawkes knelt beside them. He gathered their seizing hands and nuzzled them gently.

"Stop Korsika," Calisto said in a fraying voice. "The world's about to end."

"End-times are old hat for me, remember?" Fawkes said. "I'm not leaving you."

"Kellan?" Omen shouted. "Gillian?" He was still waiting for his friends to come back to his side, but Korsika was the one who arrived, sliding into the spot as if he belonged there. Omen looked at him—with confusion, then recognition.

"We've been waiting for this moment all our lives," Korsika said. "Me, a bit longer than you."

He handed his younger self the formula. "The secret to their boots and unfair advantage."

A quake stirred, tentative at first. Warning signals spiraled down Calisto's nerves.

Omen squinted at the formula and broke out in that self-satisfied grin that Calisto knew could only portend bad things.

The quake split the asphalt wide open, a dark rent in the earth. Calisto couldn't move from where they were curled on their side. Fawkes scrambled to pull them up.

But the earth swallowed them both.

They came out in the mists.

Calisto thumped to the ground, landing in the fabric of time.

At least it was soft.

That relief only lasted a moment. Even here, an endless rumble had taken hold. Korsika's branching left tears in the fabric, great gashes Calisto ached to sew shut, but their hands were cramped into frozen claws.

"We failed," Calisto said. "We should go back to Pocket and warn everyone before . . ." Before the valley was destroyed by a stampede of travelers? Before the consumption of late humanity spawned a time war?

"The branch isn't fully settled yet," Fawkes said. "Let's go back to that moment. If Korsika could change it, so can we."

"I can't pinpoint it again. Korsika took my time tailor abilities."

"Speaking of Korsika . . ."

He wandered toward them, nearly waltzing with delight. He touched the fabric of time with both hands, grabbing at it like it was something he could hoard and keep. "This is amazing! Truly delightful!"

"Glad you're enjoying yourself," Calisto muttered.

Fawkes massaged Calisto's hands. "We'll have to wait until your power fades out of him, and then we'll—"

Fawkes didn't finish the sentence.

The Time Wardens had arrived.

They marched in double and triple the numbers that Calisto had seen in Pocket and at the Globe. Their stark uniforms perforated the white landscape. Their faces, usually so blank, were alarming for a new reason.

They were *smiling*.

They bowed to Korsika. He stood before them in his too-tight suit, looking more than a little concerned. "What is happening?" he asked.

156

"Oh," Fawkes said. "Well, that all came together a little too late."

"What came together?"

"You can't see it?" Fawkes twisted a curl. "They thought Calisto and I were a danger to your plan, so they went to Crete to stop us. They've been following you because they *want* your branch, Korsika."

"What about their obsession with the one true timeline?" Calisto asked.

"They must have decided there was no getting back to it," Fawkes said.

Calisto's skin burst out in clammy droplets. "What did the drab warden say in the labyrinth?"

"*Travelers are unnatural, a plague upon time,*" Fawkes said, calling up the threat with misty eyes and dead-voiced accuracy. "*We fight until the timelands are wiped clean.*"

"They don't want to keep us in line anymore," Calisto said. "They want to eradicate travelers."

"It looks like they're starting with the three of us," Fawkes said, returning to the present with a touch of dark, hopeless humor. "They've gotten the branch they wanted, and they're not going to let us change it."

Calisto found more Time Wardens coming through the mists in every direction. "When do we go now? Back to ancient days?"

"I'm taking you somewhere they really can't follow," Fawkes said. "Home."

"To Pocket?" Calisto asked. "But . . ."

Fawkes shook his head. "*My* home."

They broke free of the Time Wardens and started running.

Korsika ran after them.

SIXTEEN

Fawkes rushed through the mists toward the one place that always tugged at him. With Calisto at his side, and Korsika clinging to his heels, Fawkes reached the spot where tatters of mist trickled out.

The place where humanity unraveled.

The three of them tumbled into a clearing of cedars. It felt like falling out of the highest tree branch. Fawkes had done that when he was little, studying the birds, not sure whether his arms could hold him aloft and learning in the harshest way that they couldn't.

Growing up without adults had been an interesting experience.

"I thought you were from some early pocket of existence." Calisto looked around, eyes taking in the shine of thickened gold light that had been one of Fawkes's first treasures. "This is . . ."

"After the Industrial Collapse. After what came *after* the Industrial Collapse."

"Travelers can't hike this far," Calisto said. "How are we here?"

Fawkes sat down on the trunk of a fallen tree. Rumbles from the enormous quake still reached them, though they'd grown faint with distance. "I've never met another traveler from this era—I just know I can always return. I also know the Time Wardens can't follow, because when I was little, they chased me and chased me and could never reach me here."

"Well, that's a nightmare." Calisto touched the shaggy skin of the great trees and lifted their face to the sun. "But this place is beautiful."

"I know," Fawkes said. Part of Fawkes loved it here. Another part was infinitely sad when his thoughts drifted toward his hometime. Something about coming here made him itch and ache simultaneously. "Humans aren't the best, but it's hard to live without them."

"Did you start traveling to be around other people?"

"I put the boots on because they were a gift from someone I trusted. When I mind-walked and saw myself older, I always had them on." Fawkes didn't know how much to say, how much to hold back. "I put them on to go find you."

Korsika stirred, groaning. "Are you two done with whatever doomed love scene you're playing?"

"Did he just ruin this moment?" Calisto growled. "I shouldn't be surprised at this point."

Korsika sat up and looked around in a daze. "Are we in the post-everyone times?"

"Welcome," Fawkes said.

"We're not staying," Calisto said. "Don't get too comfortable."

"Me?" Korsika asked.

Calisto shook one clawed hand in his general direction because they couldn't point a finger properly. "Yes, you! Omen Korsika! With your grand destiny! You strutted around like the most important person in the timelands and broke everything."

Korsika scoffed. "You can't believe I wanted *this*."

"It doesn't matter what you wanted." Calisto threaded their arms tightly over their chest. "You didn't listen, and now we're here."

"We can fix it, I think," Fawkes said. The grumbling underfoot was a sign that this branching wasn't set in stone yet. "We can try to change the events at the club if we can make it past the big clot of Time Wardens."

"Best of luck," Korsika said.

"Oh, I have a special job for you," Calisto said. "You're going to be our decoy."

Fawkes enjoyed watching Korsika choke on his own grandeur. "Decoy?"

Calisto paced from grand tree to grand tree. "We'll leave as soon as we can, but I'm going to need my time tailoring to return so I can get us to the right moment. And *he's* going to need a costume. Where's the bag?"

Fawkes felt his hope fall off a cliff. "A deep, deep crack opened during the quake, and it rolled in."

"Sounds like we'll just have to accept our horrible fate," Korsika said with gleeful resignation.

"Didn't I tell you that I can hide pins anywhere?" Calisto plucked a small rectangle from the pocket of their shorts and rattled it satisfyingly in the silence of the grove. "I carry an emergency sewing kit, too. I just need fabric to work with."

"A three-piece suit has so much fabric!" Fawkes crowed. "Korsika's is stolen, so I'd say it's up for grabs."

"It's a good start, but I'll need more." Calisto eyed Fawkes's outfit.

160

In the end, they laid claim to every piece of clothing that both were wearing, leaving only underwear.

"You two should make yourselves busy," Calisto said. "I have to focus."

They sewed and sewed with cramped, crooked fingers, cursing Korsika. Fawkes roamed the woods in his boxers, waving at Calisto every time he found something nonpoisonous to eat. At some point, Calisto looked across the grove and found Fawkes and Korsika in deep conversation. Fawkes appeared to be describing everything they'd learned from Kellan in their temporal lessons. And Korsika appeared to be—miraculously—*listening*.

The costume was finished by nightfall.

As the grove spun out of the sun's reach, Calisto felt how troubling it was to live past the end of civilization. The intense light that slanted through the cedars was gone, replaced by immeasurable darkness.

"How are you feeling?" Fawkes asked. "Will you be able to get us back to the club?"

Calisto flexed their fingers. The stiffness was easing. "I think so."

"How did it go with the costume?" Fawkes asked.

"It's hideous," Calisto said. "Which makes it perfect. How did it go with *that* one?"

Korsika had fallen asleep across the grove, his noxious snores drifting back to where they both sat restlessly beneath the cedars.

"I helped him, the way that Kellan helped us," Fawkes said.

"With his time power? The siphon?" Calisto shuddered. "Wait, can he use it on the wardens?"

Fawkes shook his head. "They're not natural travelers, so he can't steal anything from them. But I thought with an anchor he might be able to focus his power differently, like I do with my mind-walks. We came up with something to try in the mists."

"You and Korsika?"

"He's ridiculous when he's scared, but he says he wants to help." Fawkes shrugged. "We're going to need everything we have against the Time Wardens."

The night grew colder notch by notch.

"We should leave," Calisto said.

"There's one more thing I'd like to do before we throw ourselves at danger," Fawkes said.

"So you do notice when things are dangerous!" Calisto said.

"Of course I do." Fawkes touched Calisto's lips. "If this isn't the moment . . ."

Calisto rushed forward and kissed Fawkes.

They pulled back enough to check his eyes for mist, but they looked perfectly clear. And a little startled.

Fawkes blushed so deeply that in the dark, his skin turned indigo. "I didn't know our first kiss would happen in the hometime that I left to find you."

"Thank you for bringing me here. I can tell it's not simple."

"Oh, nothing about us is simple," Fawkes said. "Except the feelings part." He smiled, and it looked soft in the dark.

Calisto wanted to touch Fawkes's lips. So they did. They couldn't wait to kiss him again. So they did that, too. They wanted to make this moment beautiful, not just to ward off the cold and the dark but to reverberate up and down their lives, reaching all of their loneliest places. Calisto kissed Fawkes—for the third time, linearly speaking—then kissed him again, and again, until there was no separating one kiss from the next, until the numbers and the order no longer mattered. The present seemed to unspool endlessly.

High above, the ancient trees of the farthest known time stood watch.

Fawkes grazed his knuckles against his lips.

He touched them again and again, and every time, he mind-walked.

He lived those kisses so many times.

Calisto had fallen softly asleep on his shoulder. Fawkes wanted to let them rest, but the rumbling beneath the packed earth and roots was growing faint.

"Calisto," Fawkes whispered.

They leapt up as if they'd never closed their eyes. They tested their fingers. "Hardly stiff at all. Let's go."

Calisto shook Korsika awake with a firm hand.

"I had that dream where you're taking a test in your underwear, but instead of a test, it was a mad dash to save humanity," he said, groggy and not remotely moving to get up. He looked down at himself. "Oh. It was real."

Calisto dropped the costume on him. "This is for you. I never want to see . . . what do you call those?"

"Tighty-whities," Fawkes supplied.

"Never again."

"I'll come with you," Korsika said, looking over the costume. "But I'm not wearing *this*."

Calisto shrugged. "Then we won't be able to tell Kellan and Gillian that we've forgiven you for using our powers. We won't be able to mention that you were brave when it mattered the most and *might* be worth forgiving. You definitely won't get that second chance you wanted so badly that you wrecked reality for it."

Korsika sulked just like the younger version of himself. "It's too late for that."

"There's your fitting room." Calisto pointed at one of the gigantic cedar trees. "Get dressed."

Korsika muttered something and disappeared behind the trunk.

When he came back, he was wearing the strangest outfit Fawkes had ever seen. It was a fool's motley of everything Calisto had to work with: an absurdity of denim, flannel, somber grey wool, and shiny bits. Calisto had cut out the letters from Fawkes's wordy shirt, placed a few of them aside, and rearranged them to say I AM TIME TRAVEL.

"This feels like a punishment," Korsika said, picking at the outfit.

"You're not entirely wrong," Calisto said.

"And you're sure this is going to work?"

"The Time Wardens wear uniforms," Calisto said. "I made you a uniform. And a cape, since they seem to think you're some kind of royalty. Now follow me."

Calisto, Fawkes, and Korsika walked past the boundary line of the cedar grove.

They came out inside of time.

Calisto took the precious needle from their emergency sewing kit and got to work. They were careful with the frayed thread that had brought them here, treating it delicately. It connected with others, and soon Calisto was stitching with brisk confidence. Until their fingers brushed the fabric, and people in time boots were everywhere, *fighting*.

If Calisto let themself get dragged down in visions of this branch, they'd never be able to fix it. They stitched their way down the eras, swiftly approaching the moment they needed to return to. A dozen Time Wardens guarded it. They turned their forgettable faces toward the small group of travelers.

Calisto nudged Korsika forward.

He might have dragged his time boots about coming back with them, but when he was presented with an opportunity to be dramatic, he seized it. "My people," Korsika said, tossing his cape. "I'm glad you're here. We have much to discuss about this new world of ours."

The Time Wardens cocked their heads.

"*Calisto,*" they said, voices cold and ragged. "*Fawkes.*"

Calisto shivered.

"These two tried to stop me, but they're yours now." Korsika waved the Time Wardens forward to claim their prize.

As they left their posts to detain Fawkes and Calisto, they took their eyes off Korsika.

Fawkes gave him a tiny, almost imperceptible nod.

Korsika grabbed Fawkes's wrist.

Fawkes's eyes went instantly white, but Korsika's didn't follow suit. Instead, his other hand shot out, and every warden he touched stopped dead in their tracks as *their* eyes filled with mist.

"Look at your past," Korsika commanded the Time Wardens.

What he had learned in the cedar grove was this: his power didn't stop at siphoning the temporal abilities of others. With a little help, he could bridge those abilities from one traveler to the next. Together, Fawkes and Korsika were making the wardens mind-walk through nothing more or less than their own miserable choices. Strangely blank faces took on the sharp focus of memory, the weight of forgotten pain. The wardens were feeling the humanity they'd given up in order to live a half-life in the mists and hunt travelers.

For the first time in ages, they *remembered themselves*.

"It's working!" Korsika shouted. "Fawkes has to stay here, though. Go!"

Calisto rushed forward and stuck a pin in time.

They came out in that now-infamous spot behind the club in Palo Alto.

Omen was standing alone with the formula for time boots in his hand. Calisto should have ripped it up when they first saw it in the costume shop. They considered stabbing Omen in the foot with their shears and running off with it.

"You're one of *them*," Omen said, looking up from the scrap. "A traveler."

"So are you," Calisto said.

He shook his head. "I'm not like my friends. They just went who-knows-when without me."

"They're going to bring you a pair of boots. They'll teach you how to travel. You should trust me because I happen to know that for a fact." Omen stared into the fog, at the spot where Kellan and Gillian had vanished. "I need that piece of paper. You never should have given it to yourself."

"Is this what I think it is?"

Calisto nodded. "Korsika, your older self, stole it. If you keep it, so many bad things will become inevitable."

Omen wavered, studying the paper in the dim light from the streetlamps. He went to slip it back in his pocket.

"I stole my grandmother's time boots," Calisto said.

Omen looked up with a puzzled expression.

"I was afraid that she'd put them on, leave me, and never come home," Calisto admitted. "But I'm glad I gave them back. You can't steal someone else's moments. You have to find your own."

"Why would I bring this to myself if I didn't need it?" Omen asked, gripping the paper tighter. "What if this is my destiny?"

"Destiny is just a choice you haven't made yet," Calisto said swiftly, surely. "I didn't come up with that, by the way. Kellan told me. They're the one who sent me here to . . ." Calisto almost said *to stop you*. But they'd been stopping Korsika, not this much younger person who hadn't made his mistakes.

Time was branching; everything could change. That was true whether the branch was large or small, whether everyone stopped to feel its reverberations or kept moving. Every word Calisto chose in this moment mattered, just like every stitch in a garment determined what shape it would take. "Kellan sent me to help."

"Kellan? *My* Kellan?" Omen asked.

Calisto nodded.

Slowly, Omen handed over the piece of paper.

Calisto tore it into tiny pieces.

The bits were carried off on a wild crosswind that seemed to blow all the way from Pocket.

PART THREE

SEVENTEEN

Anyone who has taken a long journey knows that returning is a faster business than leaving. This is true even if the two legs cover the same distance. In Calisto's case, the journey home was more direct—and accelerated by the fact that a dozen Time Wardens were on their trail.

The wardens' ranks had shrunk to pre-branching numbers. This bundle *moved*, sure-footed within the mists where they'd lived for so long.

"Calisto!" Fawkes shouted. "Hold on!" The fabric of time wrinkled underfoot, and Calisto worried that it was another temporal catastrophe—but it passed.

"What was that?" they asked. "An aftershock?"

Fawkes shrugged.

"Where's Korsika?"

Fawkes shrugged harder. "I turned to look right before that ripple happened, but he was gone."

"He probably ran away," Calisto said. "To avoid any more consequences."

They didn't have time to track him down. They kept running from the Time Wardens, using the last of the thread from Calisto's tiny sewing kit, bolting through time as fast as their cramped fingers could manage. Somewhere around the 1920s, they realized that it wasn't going to help.

Calisto dropped the needle.

"What are you doing?" Fawkes asked. "They're very much on our heels."

"*Fawkes,*" the Time Wardens chanted. "*Calisto.*"

"I hate when they do that," Fawkes said.

"Being the time tailor means I can find a moment in the timelands, but Pocket isn't *in* the timelands," Calisto said. "Besides, I don't want to lead them there. And I'm not hiding anymore."

They were going home.

They thought of Mena heading back to the mountains because the beauty of that place still pulled at her. They thought of Kellan in their adopted ancient land. Richard and Tiye, wandering into Pocket and fashioning a life, making it their own. Nori, who had always loved the place she was from. And Fawkes, from everywhen and nowhen, a lonely figure set adrift in time. Only to find his way home to Calisto.

They closed their eyes and let their feet lead them the rest of the way.

Fawkes loved this part.

"Calisto, you don't want to miss this."

The mists gave way to a view of a green valley dotted with candy-bright houses. The crosswinds of change blew strong as Fawkes led them over the hills. With a few confident steps, their feet left the ground far below. Impossibly far.

Fawkes held Calisto's hand tight.

"Are we *flying*?"

It was a powerful and yet untethered feeling, to fly. But to fly with someone who was doing it for the first time?

This was a new treasure.

Fawkes and Calisto sailed over Pocket, the whole valley cupped like a palm, the roads crisscrossing it. They reached the market and drifted down like leaves on gentle switchbacks of wind.

Below their feet, people's faces were upturned, watching.

Fawkes and Calisto landed softly in front of the Inn of All Ways. Calisto held on to Fawkes for a few extra moments, until they felt certain of the ground. A light rain of applause fell from the impromptu crowd, and then everyone returned to their business. Besides the wild winds, all was usual at the all-weather market.

Calisto ran into the Inn of All Ways, half expecting to find the town gathered for an emergency meeting. They were greeted by booths of travelers and the smell of strong Turkish coffee. "Everything looks . . . like it always does."

"Where do we go next?" Fawkes asked.

Calisto knew exactly where—and not just because Fawkes was still in his boxers. Their feet led them down the east road. Costumes for Time Travelers had its door wide open to the morning air. Inside, it was properly busy, three travelers waiting to be fitted.

The costumes were exactly where they should be. There were no heaps on the floor. The racks were lined with hanger after hanger, each one laden with a pristine outfit, the long window filled with gorgeous displays.

"Calisto!" Mena bustled out of the back with an armload of fabric and dumped it on her cutting table. She gave Calisto a measuring look—from the time boots to the ripped jean shorts to the belt lined with sharp objects. "When in the world have you been? What is this costume? Did a tornado dress you?"

Calisto flew at Mena, half tripping over the floorboards to get to her faster. They nearly smothered her with a hug. "You're back! You're safe! You're working already?"

"The work piles up when nobody's here. Of course *I'm* safe. I went home for a quick trip. When I came back, *you* were gone, no way of knowing when!"

Calisto had the keys to the shop still hanging on their belt. They started to unloop them. "Keep those," Mena said. "You think I gave you the only set? I made those for you."

"You're not mad about the shop?"

"Mad, why?" Her hands flew like uncaged birds. "That you closed *my* shop when travelers needed costumes?" Mena frowned until her face buckled. "You work so hard, I can't be mad. But tell me if you want to leave. Don't make me worry. You're not the only one who worries, you know."

Calisto spun around to look at the perfectly intact costume racks. "Everyone must have fixed it up before you got home."

"Fixed it? From what? Did you hit your head while you were traveling?"

Mena's eyes landed on Fawkes's general state of undress. "Look at you! I can't decide if it's good you came into my shop, or if this is the most scandalous thing my old eyes can remember. Either way, we'll get you something to wear. Fitting room!"

"Mena, did someone come to Chieti and warn you about the Time Wardens?"

"Time Wardens?" Mena spit over her shoulder three times. "No one has heard from those fascisti in ages."

Calisto pulled Fawkes into the racks. As much as they wanted to press him into the fabrics and kiss him, there were other matters at hand. "What is happening?"

"I thought you'd be happy to be home," Fawkes said. "Mena seems nice!"

"*Nice* is not the first word anybody would use," Calisto said. "Or even the dozenth. She's acting like the Time Wardens never came through looking for you and wrecking the place and trailing Korsika."

"Korsika," Fawkes echoed. "This has something to do with him disappearing in the mists, doesn't it?"

"*Korsika,*" Calisto cursed.

They stuck their head out of the racks. "Have you heard of a traveler named Omen Korsika?"

"It rings a faraway bell," Mena said. "What a name. Like bad things coming on the wind."

"You have no idea," Calisto said.

There was one way to confirm that Korsika hadn't blown through Pocket after the moonful festival.

Fawkes and Calisto cut across town, everyone blatantly watching. Fawkes had been given the run of the costume shop. Mena wanted to make him something bespoke, of course, but due to his near-nudity she let him pick whatever he wanted in the meantime.

She only acted a little put out when he combined pieces from six different eras.

Calisto had kept their jean shorts, ripped tights, dirt-crusted waistcoat, and sharp, shiny belt. It wasn't an outfit befitting a tailor's assistant, and Mena clearly disapproved, but wearing these clothes kept Calisto tethered to the reality of what had just happened.

A reality that seemed to be slipping away.

They arrived at the temporal cobblers.

"Have you been in here before?" Calisto asked.

Fawkes shook his head.

"You might be the only traveler alive who's never crossed this threshold," Calisto said. "This is the first place new travelers are sent after they arrive in Pocket, with their shoes from the timelands in tatters."

"What about the ones who show up barefoot?" Fawkes asked.

Calisto had never thought about them before. "It can't be pretty."

They opened the door and waved Fawkes in behind them.

"These are all *new* time boots?" He touched a heeled green pair with reverence.

"Yes, but I need a cobbler." Calisto crossed the workshop, leaving Fawkes to bask in the beauty of brand-new boots.

While the shop had a lovely quiet hum, the workshop rang with tools in motion. Adama poured molten rubber into a mold with the concentration of a physicist doing complex calculations. Calisto could see the cobblers' powers, the distinct way they envisioned the medium of time. Maybe that was why they worked as a collective. Whether or not they knew it, they kept each other anchored.

Maybe lots of travelers had time powers, or the potential for them.

As soon as the mold was filled, Adama looked up. "You're home!"

Calisto's reverie snapped in half. "Adama, what's the last time you remember seeing me?"

Their friend gave them an off-kilter look. "The time savant whisked you away from the festival right when it was getting good." He stared through the glass to the shop, where Fawkes was basking in the existence of so many time boots, shoes from two wildly different pairs on his hands, a small pile in his lap. Calisto could tell he was eager to try them on, but there was no way Fawkes would remove his own boots. "Looks like you've been together since. I knew you went traveling, but *with Fawkes*? Your first time? Ndeye and Massamba will say you're married."

Calisto's face blushed so hot it could have burned off the mists. But Adama wasn't looking at their face. He was looking at their feet. "Where did you get those boots?"

"It's a story." Calisto was uncertain where it started and had lost any sense of how it might end. "I promise I'll tell you, although parts might be hard to believe based on how you answer my question. Has Ells met any braggadocious travelers lately?"

"*Ells!*" Adama called out.

All the cobblers stopped working, the last ring of a hammer shivering the air. The hedge witch, cobbler, and notedly cantankerous elder of Pocket looked up, face shadowed by dark glass goggles. Calisto could tell that Ells was not delighted to see them. "I'm about to set a sole. What could you possibly want?"

"Calisto has questions," Adama said. "I figured they should ask you directly."

"Not in here they shouldn't." Ells leveled a sturdy finger at

Calisto. "Only cobblers in the workshop. This is a secret and time-honored process."

"That's what I came to talk to you about," Calisto said. "Did any travelers come by and act suspiciously charming? Did your ability to make time boots vanish for a while?"

"What are you talking about?" Ells asked, then redirected the question at Adama. "What are they talking about?"

"I have no idea," Adama said. "Are you trying to get back at me for helping your grandmother? This is a bit obscure."

"I met a traveler in sweatpants and white time trainers. He swore he came here and got the secrets of time boots from Ells. If that was true, you would have lost your gift for making them, at least for a little while."

"Haven't taken a break from cobbling since I started," Ells said. "My hammer never falters, and I don't *forget* how to make boots. Some of the younger cobblers need to consult the formulas, but I carry that knowledge in here." She knocked a knuckle against the side of her head. "And it's been a while since we've made a pair of *white time trainers*. The cobblers discontinued that look and good riddance."

"Korsika wasn't here." Calisto was relieved and upset in equal measure.

Ells waved a pair of tongs. "Now, I've answered your disrespectful questions, and I'm kicking you out." She pointed through the glass at the shop. "Time savant, too."

"His name is Fawkes."

"Right, then," Ells said. "*Fawkes* can do whatever he wants in Pocket, and I wish him well, but I won't let anyone get new boots mixed up. Or dirty. Or both."

178

"Hmmm. That's all you object to?" Calisto remembered things that other people didn't—and that included the meeting of the elders where Ells had been determined to cast Fawkes as a problem. Calisto scowled at the old cobbler and looked for a particularly scathing response that would also make sense given the circumstances.

Adama leaned in toward Calisto. "Sorry. She's been intense since the Loose Association and Book Club of Elders started meeting at her house."

"What about Dr. Gillian Jacobs?" Calisto asked.

"Dr. Who?" Adama put an arm around Calisto's shoulders and ushered them out of the workshop, over to Fawkes and a small heap of time boots that he'd admired. "Let's get a drink at the market after work. I want to know what's going on. Bring Fawkes. Myri will come. We'll all catch up. A lot has happened."

Calisto could tell that their ideas of *a lot* didn't match. Adama and Myri had probably decided that they were going to tell everyone they liked each other, which everyone already knew. Calisto had to tell people that an entire branch of time had been erased, which they clearly did not know.

"Those are beautiful," Adama said, with an admiring glance at Calisto's time boots. "Even if they look like they've seen a bit too much."

Calisto brought Fawkes home for dinner.

Their family was sitting down when Calisto cracked the door. Clover found another chair, Onyx an extra plate, and Myri poured tall glasses of Tiye's iced tea for both of them. Calisto inhaled the mint and lemon balm. It smelled like *home*.

"Sit down, sit down," Richard said.

Fawkes perched on his chair like a bird ready to take flight.

"Have you had a family dinner before?" Myri asked, loading his plate with flatbread.

"Yes," Fawkes said. "A family on Atlantis took me in when I was young. I didn't stay for long."

Myri cocked her head. "I thought Atlantis was mythical."

"You'd be surprised at what turns out to be real," Calisto said.

"It's in the Mediterranean," Fawkes said. "Well, it was." Richard looked like he was about to dash to his study for a pen and paper and start writing a treatise. Calisto's siblings all trample-talked one another.

"Atlantis?" Calisto asked under the din. "Really?"

Fawkes gave Calisto a tiny shrug. "End-times."

"What's your favorite era?" Clover asked.

"What's your least favorite era?" Onyx countered.

"What's it like to travel with Calisto?" Myri asked. "Is it like sharing a room with them?"

Fawkes chewed a mint leaf and considered. "It's like the pieces of a story I knew I was going to live have fallen into the right places, and I'm walking through them and feeling each one, and they mean more because Calisto's feeling them, too." He touched Calisto's hand under the table, a quick brush along their knuckles. "Also, when we're not being chased by people, it's fun."

Calisto's parents exchanged mighty looks. Tiye nodded slowly.

"You two have gotten to know each other really well, really quickly, it sounds," Clover said.

"That's great." Myri pushed the pitcher of iced tea at Calisto with an enormous grin. "Tell me more."

Onyx tipped his chair back, and Calisto knew what he was confirming: Fawkes's and Calisto's time boots were touching.

"Next course!" Nori saved Calisto from extended scrutiny by rushing to the kitchen and bringing back a steaming bowl of rice. When she lifted the cover, the smell thickened the air. "Saffron," Fawkes crowed.

"Mena brought it home from Chieti," Nori said.

"I'm glad she found those flowers," Calisto said. "I guess they are important. She told me that's why she was going back."

"*That's* what she told you?" Nori said with a crackling laugh.

"She had a very convincing speech about crocuses."

"She wouldn't tell us the whole story until she got home," Clover said.

"Which is very Mena of her," Myri added.

"Mena *had* to go back," Nori said. "Otherwise, she never would have made it here. And we wouldn't have Costumes for Time Travelers."

Confusion prickled as Calisto stared at the brilliant yellow rice, as brightly dyed as any fabric they'd worked with. "What do you mean?"

"When your grandmother was young, she met an old woman who told her she could leave home and open a shop," Nori said.

Calisto vaguely recalled that part of Mena's story. "Right. But what does that have to do with—"

"At some point, she realized that the old woman must have been her."

"Really? How does that work?"

Tiye ladled out rice for everyone. When she reached Calisto, she smiled, but sadness moved over her face like a ripple in satin. "Some travelers visit their young selves in the timelands. Some of us have no one else looking out for us. There's no paradox. It's quite beautiful, really."

Calisto shook their head, trying to get this new information to settle. Next to them, Fawkes tugged a single curl and twirled it with finely honed intensity.

"Eat, eat," Nori said. "We don't always make a big dinner like this, but when we do, we make too much."

Calisto plowed through an alarming amount of food while Fawkes picked at his plate. The last good meal they'd eaten was on Crete, with Kellan. The roots that Fawkes had foraged in his home-time hadn't done much to stave off Calisto's hunger.

"I want to bring Mena some saffron rice," Calisto said. "There are costumes backed up several travelers deep. I can take the food over to the shop."

"I'll do it," Richard said. "You two get some rest."

Fawkes and Calisto made their way up the stairs to the small yellow room.

"Are you sure Myriad doesn't mind me staying here?" Fawkes asked, looking around and touching everything at least twice.

"Myri likes to sleep outside when it's nice," Calisto said. "She's probably in the hammock with ten books."

Calisto tried to clean up the tiny space and failed. Their whole life felt cramped with family, cluttered with *things*. Before he started traveling, Fawkes had an entire era to himself. Calisto didn't even have a bedroom. Not that they would complain, but it was a difference. And all of the familiar bits of life that should have brought Calisto comfort didn't make them feel settled. Not yet.

"I know I shouldn't be upset that everything in Pocket is better . . ."

But there was a dangling thread.

Calisto tugged at it. "What do you think happened? Why is Korsika missing from everyone's memories? Is that why he vanished in the mists? Did he somehow get everyone to forget how he wrecked things?"

Fawkes sat cross-legged on top of Calisto's blanket. "Do you remember the ripple? The aftershock? What if that was its own small branching? But it wasn't the older Korsika who created it."

"You think it was Omen?"

"He could have taken a different path after you talked to him. That explains why his older self disappeared from the mists. Why Korsika never came to Pocket after the moonful festival. He never chased me down, stole the formula . . ."

"I still feel like I met him in the costume shop, though," Calisto said. "I remember finding Korsika in 1999, and Time Wardens multiplying exponentially. If he never came to Pocket and none of that happened, wouldn't we have gotten reset, too?"

"It's not a button," Fawkes said. "It's more like a stream flowing in a slightly new direction. Think about how much stayed the same."

Calisto's mind was stuck. "I don't understand how *we* know what's different."

"Maybe because we were inside of time when the branch settled," Fawkes said.

"You're saying if we were in the timelands or Pocket, I wouldn't remember meeting you?"

"It sounds like we met anyway," Fawkes said.

"Of course we did." Calisto's mind rooted in that certainty, even as their body drifted toward sleep. "You came to the moonful festival to find me."

"We traveled together, too. Your grandmother said you left Pocket."

"That . . . is a little more surprising," they admitted.

Calisto wondered if they would have figured out their time tailor abilities in this new branching, or met a minotaur named Kellan. If they would have kissed Fawkes or if they'd still be waiting.

"I'm glad we remember our branching," Calisto said.

"Even with how dangerous it was?" Fawkes asked.

"I don't think I can pick those threads apart from the other ones." Calisto tossed aside the quilt, uselessly fluffed the thin pillows. "All of that danger did make me exhausted, though. We should sleep."

"Should I take off my boots?" Fawkes asked quietly.

Calisto was determined to help Fawkes feel comfortable. "There have been time boots in my bed before," they assured him. "Not on a person, but—"

"I want to take them off. My soles haven't been free in a long time."

"Are you sure?"

Fawkes lowered his shoulders and looked at Calisto. His brown eyes were softly illuminated. They held his loneliness, but also the past that Fawkes and Calisto now shared with each other and no one else.

"Yes. I'm sure."

"I can do it." Calisto slid off the bed and knelt in front of Fawkes, undoing the stiff knots, tugging at the heels. They had to yank the laces looser before trying again. The first boot had to be pried off one awkward inch at a time. The second came off in a flying tumble of leather and colorful sole. Fawkes removed his socks and arched his feet. Feelings shifted across his face like fast-moving winds.

"Do you think it's safe to fall asleep without them?" he asked.

"They'll be close by." Calisto lined up their time boots—both pairs—neatly at the edge of the bed. "And yes. You're safe."

Calisto rubbed a few circles into Fawkes's tired feet, his legs, his hips. Fawkes's head tipped all the way back. "That feels . . . the best."

"I thought it might. You've been traveling for a long time."

"I could travel forever if you do this," Fawkes said with a low throaty rumble.

"Resting is important," Calisto said. "Real rest, not just stealing a little sleep between destinations."

They climbed into bed.

Calisto pulled Fawkes close like in Kellan's hut on Crete, his back to their chest, perfectly matched, like a fabric and its backing. They breathed together, and each breath was a little slower than the last. Calisto smiled into Fawkes's shoulder. "Everything worked out, Fawkes. We stopped a time war. Omen probably made some better life choices. The costume shop isn't destroyed!" They kissed Fawkes's shoulder freckles. "We're here together."

Calisto reached to turn off the bedside light, and shadows sliced the room.

"Pocket is safe," Calisto mumbled as an afterthought.

They slept soundly in the narrow bed.

But Fawkes stayed awake, staring at the ceiling, missing the sky, trying to put one piece into a very important place.

/// /// ///

In the mists, the wardens stirred. They remembered everything. Travelers should not be able to branch a timeline like that.

Break a timeline.

They should not have the power to send wardens back to the timelands, to make them forget the glorious battle for the soul of time. *This* was why travelers were not allowed to walk together. To work side by side. It gave them too much power.

The wardens—who had worn uniforms for so long, they'd forgotten the shape of their bodies, who had long ago given up what they were alone to become something greater, more than a group, a many-headed creature who could survive in a place that was cold and white and erased you slowly, a place that took everything and gave back nothing—did not see a drop of hypocrisy in this.

The wardens had traded it all in service of keeping the world safe. They had traded histories and selves. They had traded home-times and families and friendships. Perhaps some of them had loved something, once. Being forced to remember had slowed them down, one more stark reminder of what mattered.

Travelers were unnatural, a plague upon time.

The wardens lingered where the mists became the valley. A misplaced scrap of world that travelers had grabbed for their own use. The wardens had always believed their numbers were too small to take this place. But they had marched into Pocket to find the time savant, and no one had stopped them.

There was no turning back for the wardens. Their branching of choice had collapsed in an instant, all of their plans erased, but they had developed a taste for a world without travelers. It was no longer enough to pick off the strange and the stragglers. A few stolen pairs of boots would not suffice.

They stirred through the mists, talking to each other, not because they needed to speak out loud to know one another's thoughts but because it soothed them, trading the same ragged whispers back and forth:

"Now is the moment to stop hiding."

"Soon, we fight."

"Until time is wiped clean."

"They will not stop us."

"Calisto and Fawkes will not stop us."

Their branching of choice had collapsed, but the wardens knew exactly who to blame.

"Calisto."

"Fawkes."

EIGHTEEN

Calisto woke up alone.

The bed, even though it was narrow, felt much too big. Myri peeked in and said, "Did Fawkes leave early?"

Calisto leapt to their feet.

Fawkes's time boots were no longer sitting by the bed next to their own. Was he leaving Pocket, traveling without them? He'd talked so much about how he wanted to find Calisto, to stay by their side.

That didn't make sense.

But nothing had quite added up since Calisto got home. They shoved their feet into their boots and ran by Myri—they'd fallen asleep in their clothes, so there was no need to change. They bolted down the stairs, lightheaded with the floating fear that they'd never see Fawkes again.

He was sitting in the kitchen, boots cleaned and re-laced, calmly drinking tea with Nori.

Calisto's heart scudded but could not slow down. "Is everything all right?"

"Your friend Fawkes just told me what you two did," Nori said quietly. "You were very brave, Calisto."

"You . . . believe him?"

"I do," she said. "I don't know Korsika, but he's hardly the first traveler to go rogue in some way. It's a good thing you two were able to get the formula back. The thought of time tourists running roughshod over Pocket is bad enough, but—" She stopped herself. "Well, I don't have to tell you what might have happened if the Time Wardens had their way. You saw it for yourselves. And after what happened to my parents, I believe that they are capable of anything."

"The Time Wardens?" Calisto asked. "But you told me—"

Nori shook her head, hands wrapped firmly around her tea mug. "The disaster I told you about was real. It happened because wardens were trying to force a branch. Your grandparents had caused a change, and they were trying to change it back. They killed your grandparents in the process."

"So the Time Wardens were responsible for their deaths." Calisto tried not to sound cold, though it crept into their voice like frost onto a windowpane. "And you didn't think it was important to tell me?"

"I thought it was important *not* to tell you! Traveling is dangerous enough. I worried that if you knew about the Time Wardens, you'd stay home forever. You'd be too afraid to make your own decision. When I was your age, I *wanted* to stay in Pocket. That's different from feeling like you can never leave."

Calisto sat down with Fawkes, across the table from Nori, hitting the wooden seat hard.

189

"It gets worse," Fawkes said. "I mind-walked forward and saw wardens attacking."

"Attacking Pocket? But the branch changed, Korsika never came here, why would they . . . ?" Calisto's questions washed away in a flood of understanding. "They were in the mists when the branching happened, too."

Fawkes's expression deadened. "They know what they lost, and they're not ready to accept defeat. They don't really do that."

"How long do we have?" Nori asked.

"I don't know, but everything looks just the same as it does now." Fawkes blinked at Calisto, stricken. "How often do you change your clothes?"

"When I'm not traveling? Every day."

"You're wearing that outfit when it happens," he said, pointing to the grubby clothes they'd woken up in.

Calisto shot back to their feet. "We have to tell everyone what's coming."

Fawkes sighed. "They won't believe it. I've tried to help people before, tell them bad things that were on their horizon, but nobody wants a stranger giving them news about oncoming doom. They laugh, or it gets ugly. Or both."

"These aren't timelands people," Calisto said. "This is Pocket. And you're not a stranger."

"To them, I am."

"We can't just wait for the valley to be destroyed."

"People literally don't remember that the Time Wardens are an urgent threat," Fawkes said.

"That's not going to help your case," Nori said, dumping the last of her cold tea in the sink. "But it doesn't mean we should ignore what's coming. I've lived in fear of the wardens for too long."

"How do we get everyone to move quickly?" Calisto asked. "The elders were being human glaciers last time."

"We skip the book club and go straight to the emergency meeting." Nori banged on the banister and shouted upstairs. "Tiye, Richard, Clover, Onyx, Myri! Wake up! We're going to ring the big bell!"

Calisto hadn't expected a Pocket-wide emergency meeting to happen in their lifetime. They certainly hadn't expected to call one. In the highest tower of the Inn of All Ways, the bell tolled as Nori put her elder privilege and strong arms to use. Fawkes and Calisto left the tower and descended to the common room. Travelers trickled down from bedrooms looking groggy. The people of Pocket flooded in through the front door. Inn workers sipped early coffees as they collected around the edges of the room.

Calisto's family had claimed spots in the dark wooden booths. There was one notable absence.

"Where's Mena?" someone asked.

"We can't wait for her to leave the costume shop," Clover said. "She'll sew until doomsday."

Fawkes and Calisto looked at each other meaningfully. "Endtimes," Fawkes whispered.

"Calisto, will you tell us what's going on?" Myri asked. "This is getting scary."

They took a deep breath. "Time Wardens are coming."

Several of the older travelers stood, their alarm rising fast. Ndeye and Massamba gripped each other's hands so tight that Calisto felt it from across the room.

"What are Time Wardens?" Clover asked.

"They hate travelers," Ells said gruffly. "They don't come to Pocket. Never have, never will."

"That's not entirely true," Calisto said.

"And it's not what anyone needs to argue about right now, Ells," Nori added in a clipped tone.

"Did you see them?" Massamba asked. "How do you know they are coming?"

Calisto looked at Fawkes. He nodded.

"Fawkes saw it happening. A piece of it."

"Who's Fawkes?" someone asked.

He raised his hand awkwardly.

"Oh," Onyx said. "Wait. The time savant can see what's going to happen?"

"More like live through it," Fawkes said. "Little bits of it."

"That's how Fawkes moves through time. All of you should understand that," Calisto challenged. "You move through time differently from other people. You've always wanted to know the truth about him, and this is it."

"I have so many questions," Myri said.

"Are you an oracle?" Salamasina asked. "I miss the old oracle."

"Why should we believe these little visions he has?" a traveler broke in. "Are they always accurate?"

A clamor burst through the room. Calisto wasn't going to let people kill the only time they had. They stood on a chair and summoned their loudest voice. "Why are you acting like Fawkes is some mysterious stranger you can't trust? *I* trust him. I have since the moment I brought him to the costume shop. He fought to keep the Time Wardens out of Pocket, even though no one here has ever fought for him. He deserved better than that. He *deserves* better."

Fawkes tugged at a seam of Calisto's many-scrap cloak, a silent thank-you.

"I wish I hadn't seen the Time Wardens, but I can't change it," Fawkes said.

"You can risk everything to pretend this isn't coming," Calisto added, "or we can prepare."

Silence settled thickly over the crowd.

"It's time for a vote," Nori said. "Raise your hands if you want to pretend."

Calisto waited as the silence stretched to the breaking point. Nobody put their hands up.

"Raise your hands if you want to prepare."

Adama put up a hand without hesitation, followed quickly by Calisto's family. The rest of the room added their hands, one by one. Even Ells raised one sturdy finger in the air.

"I believe Fawkes," Adama said. "But why are these wardens here now?"

"They wanted to start an enormous time-spanning battle, but we stopped them," Calisto said. "So they're coming here to start one instead."

"You're saying that you brought this fight home," Ells pointed out.

"Good," Tiye said. "Home is where we are most likely to win."

"Historically speaking . . ." Richard said. Nori shot him a brisk look. "Well, that's right. Let's give them a run for their money," he added, looking far too scholarly in his three-piece suit to do anything of the sort.

"Love, most people don't know what that means," Tiye said.

"We make a stand," Calisto translated.

"There are only a few dozen wardens," Fawkes said. "We have stronger numbers. If we're together, we can hold out."

"They have weapons," Ndeye mentioned bleakly.

"It's not as though we keep an armory in Pocket," Massamba said.

Calisto leapt down from the chair. "We need to get to the costume shop!"

Everyone banded together for the short trip to Costumes for Time Travelers, moving up the east road. When they reached the shop, Calisto found Mena at her cutting table, sewing like usual.

"Did you hear the bell?" Calisto asked.

"Of course I did," Mena said through a mouthful of pins. "You think I don't know what that means? You think I didn't notice you mention the fascisti when you came home? That's why I'm working double time."

"Right," Calisto said as the rest of Pocket poured into the shop. "We need everything you have to fight the Time Wardens."

Fawkes shut the door behind them and secured the lock.

Mena handed Calisto the keys to a set of long trunks with double locks in the back room. Calisto flung them open to reveal brilliantly silver swords, dozens of daggers sheathed in leather, knives of all lengths and curvatures, wickedly spiked maces, blunt canes, and clubs.

"These are extremely real and built to perfect historical specifications," Richard said.

"I don't believe in armies, and I will not touch guns, but there is no excuse for a poorly made accessory," Mena shouted from the front room.

"Are you *still* sewing?" Myri asked as the crowd quickly armed themselves.

Mena looked around at the group, arching her ancient eyebrows. "Some of you are not dressed for this fight. These wardens hate travelers, and we do not shrink in the face of that hate. We are all travelers."

"They love order, too," Calisto said. "So please be disorderly!"

Calisto's siblings cheered.

"If you're in timelands gear, keep watch," Nori said. "Let us know if you see anyone coming."

The people of Pocket rushed through the racks, draping themselves in costume pieces and piling on accessories. Calisto ran through the shop with a mouthful of pins, hemming anything that would drag. They admired the growing mélange of styles that stomped across all known eras.

Everything wild.

Everything anachronistic.

Everything unforgettable.

"Look," Calisto said to Fawkes. "You're a style icon."

"That's a new feeling," Fawkes said. "I don't know what to do with it."

Mena forced a small packet of clothing into Calisto's arms—the one she'd been sewing when everyone came in. "This, my grandchild," she said, "is for you." Calisto unfolded the simplest linen trousers and a tunic. They knew that Mena wouldn't send them out to face the Time Wardens in *underclothes*.

"And this," she said, holding up a tunic of glimmering chain mail.

"And these," she said, hefting several pieces of glowing plate armor and a golden shield.

"Mena . . ." Calisto said. "These are too lovely to fight in."

"If you must face ugliness, you face it with beauty," Mena said. "I will keep you safe the best way I can."

One of the old travelers keeping watch shouted, "There are Time Wardens marching over the hills!"

There was no more time left with the people Calisto loved, no more moments to grab on to as they rushed by like so much slippery velvet. Calisto kissed Mena's cheek and flew toward a fitting room.

Fawkes followed Calisto, lugging half the plate armor. Shut in the tiny mirrored room together, Fawkes helped them do the world's quickest change into a full knight's costume. Under any other circumstances, it would have been the most romantic moment of Calisto's life, stripping in a frenzy and then building back up with Fawkes's hands to help at every turn.

It was still *one* of the most romantic, even under such conditions.

"You should mind-travel back to this moment if we survive," Calisto said. "And enjoy it."

Fawkes blushed the color of Calisto's best crimson thread.

As they emerged from the fitting room, Mena tried to hand them a broadsword, but Calisto waved it off. They gathered up what they truly needed: shears and seam rippers, needle and thread.

Calisto surveyed the costume shop and found everyone arrayed in the boldest finery the ages had to offer.

They were all dressed up and ready to fight for Pocket.

The sound of Time Wardens moved through the town—glass breaking, doors splintering.

"We should go out there first," Calisto said. "Just me and Fawkes. Be ready to fight when we call for you."

"Calisto . . ." Nori said.

"I have to go." Calisto flung themself at Nori for a hug, which Richard and Tiye joined just as they had since Calisto was little. "I'll come back."

"You can't promise that." Nori held on to them.

"I know."

Calisto and Fawkes left the costume shop just as the Time Wardens started up the east road. Everyone else stayed stuffed in the shop, watching through the long display windows, waiting.

"Give me a hint about why we're doing it this way," Fawkes whispered.

"I have a plan." Calisto put a hand on Fawkes's shoulder. "I'll anchor you so you can move forward in time just a *little* and see how things turn out, then we can revise the plan if we need to."

"Calisto." Fawkes looked over at them with a dark divot between his eyebrows. "I'm not going to mind-walk and leave you here with wardens."

"That's sweet, but it messes up the fail-safe I built in."

"*Fawkes,*" the Time Wardens hissed as they moved up the bottleneck of the east road. "*Calisto.*" The wardens' uniforms—so intimidating in the mists—looked a little dingy and sad against the brightness of the valley, the lively hues of Pocket's buildings.

"So what's the plan?" Fawkes asked.

"You herd the Time Wardens to me as quickly as you can."

"And?"

197

"I could explain the rest, but I might talk myself out of it. We have about three moments before they reach us. We should probably kiss."

Fawkes took Calisto's hands in his and twined them into a knot. They pressed together in the middle of the street, and Calisto kissed him as if these three moments were the only ones that existed. The only ones that mattered.

The only ones left.

They didn't have a spare moment to think about how everyone they knew had witnessed all of that kissing. Right after Fawkes broke away, the first of the Time Wardens reached them.

The fight began.

Fawkes had taken a rapier from Mena's stash and used it to swashbuckle his way through a group of Time Wardens who weren't expecting trained fighters.

"All right." Calisto slid pins in their mouth to help them focus. "This is the big moment."

They threaded a needle and stitched through what seemed to be air. It thickened beneath their fingers. Again they stabbed the needle through the stuff of reality, speeding up the moment with a few quick stitches here, slowing it down with a seam ripper there.

This valley's view on time was entirely its own, perched at the edge of the mists, populated by travelers and their children and their children's children. Here, time could be seen, not just tangibly but *differently*, from a distance that allowed it to become both strange and familiar at once. Something Fawkes could walk on, and Calisto could *sew*.

"Let's see what we can do with the time powers of Pocket on our side," Calisto shouted to Fawkes.

Fawkes nodded, pushing wardens in Calisto's direction with his swordplay. Calisto disoriented a warden by speeding up time, slowed the moment down and gained the advantage while the warden pumped their arms and legs fruitlessly, sluggishly. Calisto stuck a pin in the warden's uniform and froze them in a single moment, solid as ice.

"Keep bringing them closer," Calisto said. "As many as you can."

Fawkes's eager, elegant strikes herded more Time Wardens toward Calisto. They trapped each one in a moment. They suspended wardens like bugs in amber, instant museum pieces, ugly curiosities.

A dozen more charged in behind the ones Fawkes and Calisto were already fighting.

"Too many," Calisto said.

"Travelers!" Fawkes called. "Time for your grand entrance!"

The shop door flung wide, releasing an armed and ready group dressed at the furthest borders of fashion. Calisto's family ducked and wove around wardens trapped in immovable, eternal blocks. Their siblings and parents rushed forward to meet another wave of attack.

Adama hefted a double-bladed axe with his strong cobbler's shoulders. Massamba clutched ivory-handled double blades that looked quite comfortable in his grip. Ndeye had glinting brass knuckles. Salamasina, in a bright red pa'u combined with pink wool leggings from Pocket's alpacas, teamed up with Ells in some kind of mystical potato sack. They smudged herbs into the faces of Time Wardens and kicked at their shins with time boots.

Nori, for all of the weapons at hand, gripped pruning shears.

The Time Wardens flinched at the sight of so many travelers. They were used to dealing with frightened individuals isolated by the mists, not a bright wall of resistance. The people of Pocket met the uniform hatred of the Time Wardens with sequins and swords, candy pastels and glitter bombs.

Calisto came by and froze a warden that Myri had just immobilized with a sparkly handful to the eyes.

"Break up the bundle!" Calisto shouted.

Their friends and family looked around at one another, confused.

"Don't let the group re-form!" Clover translated.

Calisto watched as travelers and Pocket-born picked the Time Wardens apart from each other, one by one.

"*They will not stop us,*" half of the wardens chanted coldly.

"*No one will stop us,*" the other half answered.

"We won't," Calisto said. "But time will do it for us." The fabric they worked felt pliable and full of possibility beneath their fingers. They moved among wardens their friends had managed to stun or incapacitate, and with a deft pin, they stranded each one in a single moment.

"The wardens always did like things to be unchanging," Fawkes said.

"Happy to oblige," Calisto said.

The handful of wardens left looked at one another, trading some kind of unspoken signal. A riot of excitement rippled through their collective ranks. They surged forward and broke the long glass windows of the costume shop. As Calisto turned, one of the wardens slipped behind them. Before Fawkes could cry out, the warden had a knife at Calisto's throat.

The ground beneath Fawkes and Calisto heaved. A new branch was coming for them, fast.

The wardens looked blankly but directly at Fawkes.

"*Fawkes,*" the one with the knife said.

"*Calisto,*" the rest answered.

Calisto's family and friends stumbled forward to save them even as the ground shook. Several fell. The Time Warden pressed the knife harder, holding out a hand to stop anyone from heroics.

"*You are unnatural,*" he chanted directly into Calisto's ear.

"*And when you are gone . . .*" the others said.

"*The rest will follow.*"

Calisto held still and tried to be patient.

Fawkes didn't know what to do, though.

He felt himself going misty. "No, no, no," he instructed himself harshly. "Not right now." But then he was gone, his mind wanting to show him a way out and running into blank white walls. He was unanchored, unmoored, his mind mixing end-time after end-time with well-loved flashes of Calisto. Calisto's quick smile, Calisto's bright pins, Calisto's knowing fingers. Their hands knotted together. Their faces so close in the dark. Calisto's warm, shifting body under the great cedars, in bed only that morning. And then— Fawkes couldn't find them. No matter where or when or how hard he looked. Calisto was gone.

He fought his way back to the moment.

When he got there, Calisto was staring at him, trying to smile.

It felt like the end. It felt like they'd barely gotten to start.

"Calisto . . ." Fawkes said, his throat closing over their name. He wouldn't let the wardens be the last ones to say it.

"Fawkes," Calisto said. "I'm glad you found me."

A great mist descended, and Fawkes watched as people's eyes went white all at once—all *but* his.

This was something new.

"Wait!" shouted a faraway voice.

Over the hills flew a brown speck the size of a flea, growing swiftly larger as it raced across the skies. A moment later, Fawkes could see a traveler wearing the shaggy pelt of a minotaur and magnificent Oxford-style time boots. Behind them flew a dapper man in a glorious mantle and a woman with a messy red bun and the neatly fitted khaki of an archaeologist.

"Kellan?" Fawkes said right as they landed.

They shrugged off the minotaur's pelt. "I had a big oracle moment, realized this was happening, and couldn't stay in Knossos to let you two handle it on your own. You're my best pupils! Well, even though we branched, and you could have forgotten me." Fawkes threw himself at Kellan in a wild hug. "I should have known *you'd* remember."

"How do we save Calisto?" Fawkes asked as Omen and Gillian touched down beside Kellan. The three of them glanced at everyone paused in the fight: misty-eyed travelers and Pocket-born and Time Wardens alike.

"They're going to come back in a moment," Kellan said, "and I can't manage that trick again. It took quite a bit of power, which Omen had to spread around a lot. He's been working on his bridging abilities—it's very impressive." Omen blushed. Kellan kissed the corner of his lips and said, "You're *also* my best pupil."

"I can slow them down and disorient them with the time words I've been gathering," Dr. Gillian said. "They have to be spoken in the right order, with great care and intention. Otherwise, it can all go a bit sideways."

"And then, Fawkes, you and Omen can work together again!" Kellan said.

"Do you . . . remember me?" Fawkes asked, looking at the dark-haired man in the robe. He both was and wasn't the traveler who'd chased him through the mists and challenged him on Shakespeare's stage.

Omen winced. "Kellan's taught themself to mind-walk through different branches of time, and these two never let me live down the way I almost, well, ruined it."

"Yes, because that would have been bad for you!" Gillian said. "As it is, you surprised me by turning out quite nicely." Gillian ruffled Omen's dark hair, and he blushed again.

The mists were lifting from everyone's eyes. "All right, Gillian, it's time for those special words," Kellan said.

As people blinked back into the present, dazed, Gillian walked through the crowd, calmly tapping the Time Wardens on the shoulders and saying, "Moribund. Unctuous. Crepuscular. Writhe. Rot."

The wardens wilted, as if each word slowed and sapped them.

The one holding Calisto faltered, dropping his grip, and Fawkes's rapier point was ready. He drove the Time Warden back, flinging the knife so far, it landed on one of the gabled roofs of the inn.

Calisto ran.

Dr. Gillian kept walking, now touching the shoulders of the people of Pocket and the travelers in their brazenly beautiful costumes. "Veritable. Evergreen. Omnipotent. Mellifluous. Wonderment. Turtle."

"Turtle?" Fawkes whispered.

"There's no understanding these things completely," Kellan whispered back.

The travelers perked up, looking like they'd woken from a long night's sleep. The fight started up again.

Fawkes fought his way over to Omen. "If I find a moment, can you share it with everyone?"

"I'd be delighted to bridge for you," Omen said, putting a hand out to Fawkes. "Shall we?"

Fawkes grabbed Omen's hand.

He left this embattled scene behind.

It was a short mind-walk—it only took a few steps to find an eventuality where they won. Fawkes could see it, plain and true. Afterward, Pocket swirled with travelers and people who made their homes in a valley away from the harshest truths of the timelands.

Everyone else could see it, too.

"This is the future," Omen intoned. "You can fight us, but you can't stop travelers forever."

Time Wardens howled like infants, and then their cries twisted, torqued. Their blank faces became blanker, draining the last dregs of whoever they once had been. Their agony rose in smokelike wails. Calisto reached out with a pin and stuck it in the air—where it stayed, freezing each Time Warden in everlasting defeat.

A final warden came running out of the costume shop, screaming, as Mena chased him.

Calisto pinned that one, too.

People walked around, inspecting the immobile bodies of the Time Wardens, the wretched poses they would hold forever. Calisto felt a strange combination of proud and exhausted and simply *done*. The terror they hadn't had room for washed over them in thick sweeps.

"What do we do with frozen Time Wardens?" Myri asked.

"We could send them back to the ancient world as a sort of horrible sculpture and cautionary tale all in one," Dr. Gillian offered.

"We could sink them with Atlantis," Fawkes said. "I happen to know when it's going down."

"We could send them back to their hometimes as utter failures and make them face horrible, menial, meaningless lives," Kellan suggested.

"Volcano?" Omen tried.

"I get the feeling that everyone will need to be part of this decision, together," Nori said.

"We'll start with a meeting of the Loose Association and Book Club of Elders," Ells announced.

"Book club?" Dr. Gillian asked, her eyes lighting up.

Calisto didn't follow the elders as they headed slowly toward the Inn of All Ways. They sat down in the dust of the east road. Fawkes came and sat, cross-legged, next to them.

When Calisto imagined what came next, this was what they chose: a mouthful of pins and Fawkes, right nearby.

"Now it's done," Fawkes said. "Pocket is safe."

"I just wish we hadn't wrecked the costume shop. Again." Calisto winced as they faced Costumes for Time Travelers. The glass was shattered, the display dress forms scattered far and wide, the door hanging by a hinge. Mena stood at the threshold, surveying the damage with a brisk eye.

Mena sighed. "We can fix it, but . . ." She walked over to Calisto, took both of their hands in her own gnarled, brisk, loving grip.

"Calisto, you're fired."

NINETEEN

The first thing Calisto did was make themself a new costume. It had a few important things in common with the one that they'd made for the moonful festival, that night when they still thought their whole destiny was as big as the borders of the valley.

There were canvas trousers, lined with deep, baggy pockets for buttons, trims, and swatches of fabric. There was a belt ringed with the sharp tools that Calisto needed for their work—shears, needles, pins. There was a waistcoat, of course, though this one was done in raw silk. And Calisto's cloak. This time, they didn't patch it together out of leftover bits from the costume shop. They spent months sourcing materials, traveling to timelands markets, bargaining in dimly lit shops, and making pilgrimages to high mountains where the best spinners and weavers of the eras worked.

This cloak was the stuff adventures were made of.

It sang out in so many colors, a waterfall flowing in wild overlapping streams: gold and silver, persimmon and jade, cobalt blue and the vivid violet of a saffron crocus. Calisto gathered the last of those fabrics in the Renaissance. On an autumn dawn in the Quattrocento, Calisto stood on a mountainside overlooking Chieti. The mist was thick and plentiful. So were the flowers. They looked endless, but they would only live for a short snip of a moment, and then they would be gone.

Fawkes gathered armfuls. Together, they carried them back to Pocket, and Mena staunchly *did not* cry. "I thought I'd never see these again." She'd hung up her time boots on a peg in the costume shop. She put the crocuses on the front counter and kept them alive for a shockingly long time.

Calisto's first official job as the time tailor of Pocket was dropping Kellan, Omen, and Dr. Gillian Jacobs back in the right moment on Crete.

The three stayed in Pocket for a while after the battle, where Dr. Gillian reveled in the unparalleled dictionary collection at the wordhouse. In the end, they all wished to go back to their chosen home. They'd found a life that suited them: Kellan ran the oracle business with a side of monster work, Gillian studied phonemes of ancient languages as they evolved in real time, and Omen kept their spacious whitewashed hut swept and cared for, when he wasn't taking long philosophical walks on the beach, dreaming up complex equations and staying far away from the temptations of capitalism.

"Come visit anytime," Kellan said.

"And thank you," Omen added.

"For getting you out of those sweatpants?" Calisto asked. "You're welcome."

"For what you did," he muttered down to his time boots— actually Greek sandals with dark-rainbow soles.

"The wardens were too ready to take advantage of Omen's insecure plan to become Mr. Time Boot," Gillian said.

"Mr. Time Boot?" Omen's eyes flashed with a furious nature that made Fawkes take a few steps back and Calisto reach for the shears.

"Oh, stop," Kellan said, making Omen wince at his own absurdity. "It's the truth. You tried to sell everyone time travel. When we're afraid, it's shockingly easy to default to the worst behaviors of our hometimes."

"You healed my timeline," Omen admitted. "And I'm sorry for what that other version of me did to you. He seems to be, well, my worst possible outcome."

"I'm glad you don't have to live with Korsika, either," Calisto said.

Fawkes and Calisto worked their way down to the beach.

"I wonder if there are other ways to heal how things have unfolded," Fawkes said as they went swimming in the wild blue waters of the Mediterranean, only to come up deep in the fabric of time. "Ways we haven't even thought of yet."

"It's a good idea to explore," Calisto replied, "especially since the Time Wardens hated it so much."

"And now they're resting at the bottom of the sea forever," Fawkes reassured them both. In the end, the elders had liked Fawkes's proposal to sink the frozen travelers along with Atlantis, and all of Pocket had voted in favor.

/// /// ///

When Fawkes and Calisto arrived back in the valley, their first stop was the temporal cobblers.

Adama was busy making time boots for Fawkes.

"They're nearly ready," Adama said. "You're absolutely sure you want replicas of the ones you're wearing, not something new? I'm working on all sorts of prototypes."

"Exactly like these." Fawkes pointed down to his well-loved and ever-dirty boots. "Can you make those, too?" He pointed at Calisto's boots, which they'd cleaned and shined enough to see the flowers—crocuses, of course—tooled in the leather along the sides.

"All right," Adama said with a slight shrug. "They're your feet."

Calisto had assumed Fawkes wanted a new—and yet identical—pair to replace his old ones. "Why do you need a replica of *my* boots, Fawkes?"

Fawkes shrugged in a way that let Calisto know there was more to the story, but he wasn't quite ready to share it.

As Fawkes and Calisto left, they saw someone hanging around the shop, pretending to inspect the thick soles of a pair of platform time boots.

"Myri," Calisto said. "I can see you waiting for Adama."

Their sibling blushed. "Well, then you can also get used to it. I've liked him for ages, and I'm not hiding it."

Calisto took Fawkes to the dumpling stall and then to the Inn of All Ways for Turkish coffee. Then they sat together on the green at the all-weather market. Fawkes put his head in Calisto's lap, and they ran both hands through his hair while they waited for Fawkes to formulate whatever it was he needed to say.

He mind-walked away, then came back. Calisto found that it didn't disrupt their moments in the way that it used to—now it was woven through Fawkes like any other part of him. And it kept things from ever being boringly predictable.

"Where were you?" Calisto asked.

"My childhood," Fawkes said.

"Hmmm," Calisto said. "I feel like you've been mind-walking there a lot since the battle."

Fawkes picked at the dumplings. "Now that I'm not being chased all the time, I've been able to sit still long enough to understand some things." He shrugged. "I feel silly for not seeing it sooner."

"Things take their own time to come together," Calisto said.

"You know how Mena went back and gave her younger self a message?"

"Yes," Calisto said, thinking of how different and empty their life might have been without Mena and the costume shop. They shivered and shrugged off the too-tangible feeling of that other life.

"I think I have to do that, too," Fawkes said.

"Send yourself a message?" Calisto asked. "Or . . . give yourself time boots?"

As they said it, the rest of the truth unfolded.

Fawkes had once told Calisto that the only grown-up in his hometime looked like him. They had wondered if that hazy and half-forgotten figure was one of his parents, but now they could see it was simpler than that.

The grown-up was Fawkes.

"It's more than leaving a message or dropping off a pair of boots," Fawkes said as Calisto's hands ran swiftly through his hair. "The small version of me has to trust *me* enough that when I leave the boots behind, I know small Fawkes will use them."

Another thought dawned on Calisto. "You bring my time boots, too. And give them to yourself to give to me later." They took a bracing swig of tea, the enormity of this task dawning. "How long will you stay with . . . yourself? We just started traveling together."

Fawkes turned skittish and shy, and it threw Calisto all the way back to the night they'd met. "The grown-up . . . *I* . . . wasn't always there. So I don't have to be there continuously. But someone needs to take care of small Fawkes. I needed that. It kept me going." He shrugged. "I'm all I had."

"I'm going to help," Calisto said with a single, certain nod.

"I don't want you to pause your life," Fawkes said.

Calisto stood up, grabbing for their pins. "Fawkes, this *is* my life. I'm a time tailor. I can find any moment you need."

Fawkes's smile was a wide, unbroken string.

Fawkes found himself playing under the trees, alone.

The smell of cedars filled his nose, fresh and sharp. Sunlight had a smell here, and it got caught in the needles. Light came down in thick, solid beams. It fell on a tiny child with dark curls, crouched low to the ground, poised with nervous grace, holding very still.

Fawkes thought he was watching himself—the grown-up— emerge from the fog that laced the forest. But then he heard rustling behind him and turned. A fox was passing through the grove, flashing its fire-colored coat.

The child held their breath.

Fawkes didn't remember this moment, but he could tell that the child was trying to keep it.

And he was here, so he'd gotten it back.

Fawkes uncurled his hand and gave a small wave, trying not to startle the child. They straightened up, looked around, confused to no longer be alone.

"Hello," Fawkes said in six different languages. Then he pointed at the fox and named it in six different languages.

The child repeated them all back with fluid ease.

"Fox," they said at last. "Fox."

"Yes. Fawkes."

Soon, there were visits to other parts of his earliest history, a landscape of strange solitary eras. He taught the child how to forage, and the child reminded Fawkes where to find the clearest nooks in the stream for washing and drinking. They sat and made a fire, Fawkes sparking the tinder he'd brought from Pocket, then slipping it into the child's hand like a treasure. They played word games together into the long, dark nights. Fawkes watched over the child while they slept—their first unshattered nights of sleep.

When Fawkes left, striding into the fog or past a grove of giant trees, Calisto was always waiting.

Back in Pocket, things were changing quite a bit for a valley outside of time. For one thing, there's a new shop tucked on the west road just beyond the all-weather market. This is the home of Pocket's time tailor, who can pin down any particular moment you might need, and a part-time oracle, who can help you understand your time powers. Together, they show travelers how to move in pairs and small groups. Together, they are changing how lonely it is to walk through time.

The shop is known as Anywhen.

For another thing, Mena's eyes have gone a bit blurry from all that midnight sewing, and she finally took on a new apprentice— a traveler who worked in 1930s Hollywood before taking one too many turns on a labyrinthine set and finding her way to Costumes for Time Travelers.

"She's got a flair for it, I give you that," Mena said, then went back to grumbling. "But she's nowhere near as dedicated as you were."

"Maybe you should learn from your assistant and try taking a few breaks," Calisto said, lighting the lamps.

They felt bad, sometimes, for staying so busy with their own shop and traveling with Fawkes. Mena was starting to say things like "I won't be around forever," and Calisto was starting to believe it without putting up *too* much of a fight.

"Are you sure you don't need me in Pocket more often?" Calisto asked.

"You keep traveling, or I'll fire you again," Mena said, snipping a thread.

"I don't work here," Calisto pointed out. "I'm helping because the moonful festival is tonight."

"Yes, and soon Fawkes will come and you will go, and I will stay here and sew, because that is what this very old person wishes to do, and you would not deny me my last wish. Especially because you broke the rules of my shop."

Calisto did not think Mena would ever let them forget it.

As dusk fell, Fawkes rang the bell of Costumes for Time Travelers, dressed in a bright green velvet suit that Calisto had made for the occasion. He'd added a silk scarf from an entirely different era that made Mena clutch her heart—a bit of ridiculous playacting, since the two loved each other so quickly, it was strange to think of a time when they hadn't known each other.

Fawkes kissed Mena's cheek.

He admired Calisto's outfit, touching the places where the pieces met in raised lines. "You've always been like this." His smile was bright with memory. "With your seams on the outside."

They threaded their arms together and readied to walk beneath the light of many moons. Their matching steps broke when Fawkes's eyes went misty. He came right back.

Calisto asked, "Where did you go?"

Fawkes rocked shyly back on his heels and tipped forward to kiss Calisto.

"You two, always like this!" Mena cried, then grumbled her way to the back room.

Fawkes kept kissing Calisto because that was what he'd mind-walked into, and kissing *now* added to the lovely dark rippling of it, time doubling over on itself in the best way.

They were making the most out of falling in love not-strictly-in-order.

And somewhere, somewhen, they still are.

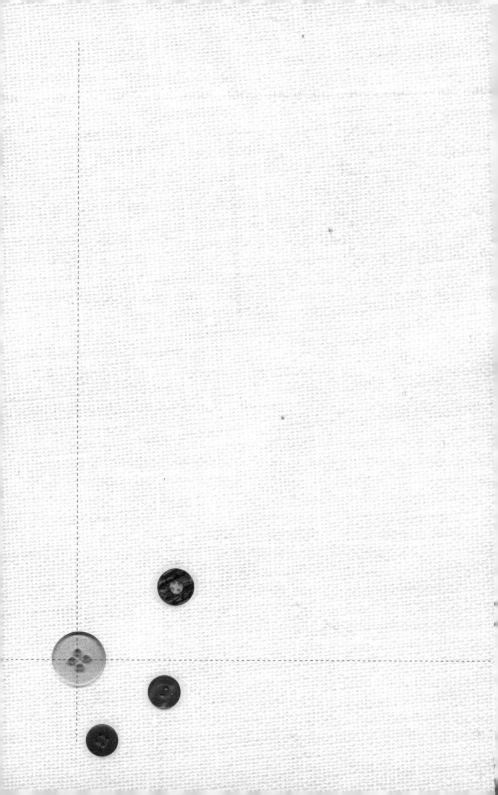